Mail-Order Brides Of The West: Evie

Other Books by Caroline Fyffe

Prairie Hearts Series

Where the Wind Blows
Before the Larkspur Blooms
West Winds of Wyoming
Under a Falling Star
Whispers on the Wind
Where Wind Meets Wave
Winter Winds of Wyoming
~~~*~~~

Colorado Hearts Series

Heart of Eden
True Hearts Desire
Heart of Mine
An American Duchess (Spin off Series)
Heart of Dreams
~~~*~~~

McCutcheon Family Series

Montana Dawn
Texas Twilight
Mail-Order Brides of the West: Evie
Mail-Order Brides of the West: Heather
Moon Over Montana
Mail-Order Brides of the West: Kathryn
Montana Snowfall
Texas Lonesome
Montana Courage
Montana Promise
Montana Reunion
~~~*~~~

Stand Alone Western Historical

Sourdough Creek
~~~*~~~

Stand Alone Contemporary Women's Fiction

Three And a Half Minutes

Mail-Order Brides Of The West: Evie

A McCutcheon Family Novel

Book Three

Caroline Fyffe

Dedicated to my dear sister, Jenny Meyer, with love.

Chapter One

St. Louis, Missouri, 1886

Evie Davenport hurried around the parlor, feather duster in hand. With a happy little skip, she flicked the implement gracefully back and forth over the walnut coffee table, then lightly fluffed the delicate glass beads dangling from the shade of the pink-and-white lamp atop the piano. A warm excitement swirled within her. A new girl was arriving today, coming all the way from Kentucky. A mail-order bride-to-be.

How romantic.

She always loved when a prospective bride knocked on the door for the very first time, her face aglow with excited anticipation.

Evie glanced at the stately grandfather clock and picked up her step. The house must be perfectly prepared when the new boarder arrived, particularly her bed, freshly made with ironed linens, and a vase of roses beside it.

Pulling the white cleaning cloth from her shoulder, Evie wiped the parlor windowsill, glancing at the roses in the garden, then moved to the mantel over the large fireplace. The burning knot that usually wedged itself in Evie's heart whenever she dreamed about love wasn't there today, and she knew why.

She paused, closed her eyes, and leaned her head back against the parlor's green-and-brown striped wallpaper. Lovingly, she ran her hand over her apron pocket, thinking about the secret posts carefully tucked away inside. She didn't dare leave them about where someone might stumble across them, but carried them with her always.

Glancing to the doorway to make sure she was alone, she drew out the most recent, and for the hundredth time, studied the return address carefully printed in the upper left-hand corner. Chance Holcomb, General Delivery, Y Knot, Montana.

Her heart fluttered, and she suddenly felt warm and tingly. A multitude of butterflies hatched inside her tummy and took flight. Why not, indeed, she thought, pushing a tendril of curly blond hair off her forehead with the back of her hand.

Evie was already twenty-two. She longed to be a bride, a wife, a mother. Even though her household duties kept her out of the kitchen much of the time, she did cook, a little—a *very* little. But she *could* keep a home beautifully, she reminded herself. No complaints there. She ran her finger lightly, adoringly, over Chance's name, imagining his face from the vague description he'd sent. Tall, twenty-seven years old, cattle rancher, light brown hair, green eyes.

The sound of laughter in the kitchen startled her from her daydreaming. Today the girls were learning how to dress a newly butchered and plucked chicken. Passing the doorway of the large, bright kitchen, she stopped and glanced inside, aching to join the fun.

Her heart sank at the disarray before her eyes. Earlier, she'd had the place spick-and-span. She'd taken extra time with the pie safe and cupboard, as well as the rectangular table in the alcove, polishing Mrs. Seymour's fine furniture to a high sheen. The room had fairly sparkled. Now, trying to find one area that wasn't a mess was a challenge. In addition, the back door to the vegetable garden and rose walk stood open like an invitation to any fly that might be passing by. Feathers fluttered on the warm spring breeze, dancing around the yard like baby lambs.

Heather Stanford, an orange feather stuck to her nose, stood back as she watched Angelina Napolitano, always a take-charge kind of girl, grip the poultry by a plump drumstick and stuff the medium-sized hen into an earthen pot. Angelina clanked the lid down tight, flashing a triumphant smile.

"Very good, Angelina," Mrs. Seymour said from behind her. "Remember, girls, you will want to baste your chicken with butter every ten to twenty minutes to keep the meat moist and turn the skin a nice golden brown."

The matron's gaze roamed the room, touching the face of each young woman. Her brown hair, silver-streaked at one temple, was done up in a bun and her dress complemented her trim figure.

"One of the fastest ways to a man's heart is through his stomach. I can't stress that enough."

Mrs. Seymour, owner of the Mail-Order Brides of the West Agency, and Evie's employer ran a tight ship. She was tall and dignified, if not a bit weathered for her forty-some-odd years. Girls of high moral standing, with good domestic abilities, were her trademark.

As a fatherless girl—an illegitimate child, Evie corrected in her mind—Evie herself could never be considered a proper candidate to be a bride. Mrs. Seymour avoided the subject assiduously, clearly wanting to spare Evie's feelings. She knew she was different, and had taken the hint. At these thoughts, a small bubble of shame tried to steal away her happiness, but she refused to let it.

When Mrs. Seymour caught her eye, Evie quickly stuffed the post back into her pocket and smiled a bit too brightly. What would happen if the matron found out she'd taken the letters without permission? And—had gone so far as to answer them! She swallowed and took a deep, calming breath.

"Are you finished, Evelyn?" Mrs. Seymour asked evenly. It wasn't that Mrs. Seymour was unkind. On the contrary, when Evie's mother had died eight years ago, Mrs. Seymour had cared for her with all the devotion of a second mother. But as grateful as Evie was to her for her job and room and board, her heart ached for more. A home of her own. A man to love. Children in her arms. If she didn't take matters into her own hands, she would likely be stuck here forever.

"Almost, ma'am. I'm going to make up the new girl's bed right away, then all I have left to do is shake out the rugs."

Prudence Crawford, a mean-spirited girl if there ever was one, gave a smirk, boldly looking down her nose at Evie. She had been at the agency for ten weeks, an unusually long time for a bride-to-be, and never missed the chance to make Evie feel small. Her black hair, pulled back in a severe bun, made her look older than her twenty-five years. After making sure her haughty look had registered on Evie, her eyes widened with false innocence.

How can anyone be so unkind? Turning to go back to work, Evie stopped at the sound of Trudy Bauer's voice. "The flowers you put in the dormitory yesterday were just lovely,

Evie. Thank you so much. I hadn't seen the pink ones until you brought them inside. They're my new favorite." Trudy smiled warmly.

Evie smiled. "I'm glad you liked them." Trudy didn't know, but she was Evie's best friend. Even though Trudy had only been at the agency for two weeks, the young woman had endeared herself to Evie in so many ways. She made her feel special. Appreciated. She'd gone out of her way several times to seek her out and chat over some amusing story.

If Evie had ever had a sister, she'd want her to be just like Trudy, with her high spirit of adventure and bubbly personality. And, even better, Trudy took delight in volleying back a kind remark to each of Prudence's mean ones. The back and forth had actually turned into a game of sorts, and everyone besides Mrs. Seymour noticed. Heather nodded and smiled her support, and Kathryn winked.

Evie hurried off. How surprised everyone would be if they learned *she* also had a handsome husband-to-be, waiting impatiently for her arrival—for no matter how modest Chance tried to come across in his letters, she *knew* by the things he said that no Prince Charming could be as sweet, or as handsome. Chance Holcomb, with a newly constructed home on a ranch outside the small, untamed town of Y Knot, Montana.

At least, that's what Chance had called it, giving her the opportunity to back out of the arrangement if the setting sounded too remote for her taste. Small was fine, but remote worried her a little. Anxiety tickled the back of her mind.

Evie's least favorite thing on earth was black with eight legs. Large or small, it didn't matter. Her fear of spiders was blind, uncontrollable. The spindly, evil-looking creatures terrified her.

"Here we go, sweetness," her mother said, reaching out her arms as Evie lay sleepy-eyed in her warm bed after a midmorning nap. "I'm sure you're as hungry as your chubby rag doll." Her mama's smile suddenly vanished and her eyes grew wide. A shriek ripped from her throat! She shrieked again, sending Evie's heart shattering into a million tiny pieces. What was wrong? Did her mother hate her? The door to the nursery banged open. The man she knew only as the Colonel rushed in. Her mother pointed straight at her. Had she turned into a monster while she'd been dreaming of strawberry pie?

It was her earliest memory. One that haunted her dreams every few months.

The Colonel reached out, his large hands getting closer. He jerked back, then came forward again. Scooping her hair between his hands, he threw something to the floor and stomped on it. She began sobbing uncontrollably. Then she found herself in the warm arms of her mama, clutched tightly to her chest. A black widow had crawled into her hair as she'd slept.

Evie took a deep, calming breath to settle her nerves, then descended the stairs into the basement where the laundry service had left the clean linen. After the spider incident, she used to pretend the Colonel was her papa, who loved her, and took care of her. If she let herself wonder about her real papa, it pained her deep inside, and her head ached. She would crawl under her blankets until the hurting went away.

So, like now, she pushed the hurtful topic out of her mind, and turned to other, safer subjects, like Chance, like a new life in Montana, like a home of her own.

In his last letter, Chance had shared his desire for a wife, a partner, someone to help him build his dreams, their dreams. His few words were lovely, expressing his feelings better than she had at most times. He did say he hoped she could cook a few hearty meals, nothing fancy but staples to keep his belly full while working the ranch.

Guiltily, she snatched up the bedding and climbed back up the stairs. She'd avoided that issue altogether, and he hadn't asked again, probably presuming her silence meant she could handle a kitchen just fine. He'd cautioned the territory was rough, and wild, but promised to take care of her to the best of his abilities. Chance had sent her passage money in his last letter. Her only concern was Mrs. Seymour's reaction.

Would the matron object? She wouldn't stop her from going after all the arrangements had already been made, would she? She couldn't possibly do something like that, or could she?

Chapter Two

Chance Holcomb let the door of the mercantile slam behind him, then strode down the boardwalk, frustrated as all get-out. The fifty-pound crate of nails he'd ordered, as well as hinges and other hardware, hadn't come in for the third week in a row, bringing the construction of his house to a screeching halt. Something about a labor problem in St. Louis.

He stopped, stepped back, and let several women breeze past, politely touching the brim of his black Stetson.

He glanced around. Y Knot was quiet. A few horses stood in front of the saloon, another at the leather shop next door. A puff of wind picked up some dirt from the middle of the street, forming a small dust devil. The swirling funnel twirled away, zigzagging as it went.

After years of riding for the McCutcheon spread, Chance had finally taken part of his lifelong savings and most of a modest inheritance received two years ago from an aunt in Boston—an aunt he hadn't known he had—and purchased a tract of land he'd been looking at for ages.

Not a huge spread, but enough to get a man started. Then he'd gone out looking for something special to raise there. If he couldn't compete with the Heart of the Mountains on quantity, perhaps he could in quality. Give the ranchers, and the stockyards in Cheyenne, something different. Something they'd never seen before. A little friendly competition was good for the soul.

Keeping just enough money back to build a house, a barn, and a couple of outbuildings, he'd traveled to Wyoming to inquire about a breed of cattle he'd heard about some years back in a saloon there. The Charolais. From France. They were large boned and wide-eyed, and the meat, low in fat, was considered superior overseas. If he could be one of the first ranchers to breed them, and later cross them with Herefords, he just might be able to make a decent living—perhaps even more.

It took some doing, but he'd finally located the rancher with the pretty French wife he'd met way back then, who was breeding Charolais. Now ten fine-looking blond heifers and one breeding stock two-year-old bull had the run of his acreage. All ten heifers were in calf to the original rancher's bull, and would begin calving at any time. A sense of pride ran through Chance just thinking about it.

His plan would take a handful of years and a lot of hard work until his herd was large enough to begin cross breeding. Until then, he'd keep all the heifers, sell off the bull calves good enough for breeding, and castrate the rest for market. Living would be slim for a while, but if his idea panned out— no, when it did—he felt in his gut ranchers would come from far and wide. Buy into his foresight of the rapid-growing, easy-calving bovine. When he needed the Hereford bull for crossing with his stock, he'd go to the McCutcheons.

He closed his eyes. Soon there would be ten light-colored calves roaming in the pasture, eating grass, and butting heads. Was Evie an animal lover? What would she think of the—

"I got your bride mended. Any time you want to pick her up…"

What did he just say? Chance snapped straight. Looked around.

Mr. Herrick had stepped out of the leather shop across the street and was looking at him curiously. "Are you asleep on your feet, son? Maybe you need to stop burning that midnight oil. I *said* your bridle is ready anytime you want to pick it up. It'll cost ya two bits."

Chance laughed. "That's a steal. I'll be over later. Any news from Trent?"

"Nope. Still waiting on a letter."

A moment passed. What could he say? The old man shrugged and a look of hurt crossed his face, then he shuffled back through the door.

Through the plate glass window, Chance watched as his friend went about arranging the saddles, bringing them closer to the glass. The leather smith and his son, Trent, had befriended Chance and his father when the two of them had first ambled into Y Knot, back when the place was just a one-street town. When Chance's father passed on, Mr. Herrick made a point of seeking Chance out, checking on him.

The bell in the tower clanged four o'clock, bringing him out of his reverie. He needed to get back to the ranch. He'd promised Evie a house. She was counting on him. It was one of the stipulations of the agency. If a man wanted a wife, he had to have a house, not a tent or ramshackle shack, to bring her home to.

If not for the nail debacle, he'd now be putting the finishing touches to that house. Per his request, Berta May had sewed up some lacy curtains for the kitchen window, and a thick coverlet filled with goose down for their bed. Problem was, he didn't have a place to put them yet. He wanted the house to feel homey. Welcoming. Right now the place didn't even have a roof overhead.

Still, he'd been living in the half-finished structure, his bedroll on the floor next to the expansive bed frame he'd crafted from twenty-year-old lodge pines growing on his land, *their land,* just for Evie.

The corner of his lip lifted. The agency had another stipulation, too. No consummation of vows for at least a month, a sort of get-to-know-each-other time. Unless, of course, both parties chose to forgo that stipulation. A man could only hope.

He shook his head, then started down the boardwalk toward the livery to pick up his horse and wagon. Mr. Lichtenstein, proprietor of the mercantile, had assured him he was doing absolutely everything possible. Each week that the order came back incomplete from St. Louis, the merchant felt worse. He assured Chance if there were any nails to be found, he would find them. *They just won't get here in time for me to fulfill my commitment to Evie. I hope she likes looking at the stars.*

As he walked, mulling over his problem, he passed a few strangers standing in front of the telegraph office, then Dr. Handerhoosen, going into his one-room medical building. He'd promised Evie a place where she'd be safe and warm before the winter set in. Told her the house was done—because he believed it would be. The building plan crinkled loudly when he clenched his fist in irritation. Lying, even unintentionally, was not a good way to start a marriage.

"Chance," a voice called out.

He stopped. Turned. Luke McCutcheon was riding up the street with the afternoon sun at his back.

Luke dismounted and tied his horse to the hitching rail. "Thought that was you. Haven't seen hide nor hair of you in a while. How're those sandy-haired heifers? Any calves yet?"

"Luke. Good to see you."

As much as he respected Luke, he didn't want to share his predicament just yet. A delay in construction wasn't the end of the world, although Evie might think different. And, anyway, he knew the McCutcheon ranch as well as the next ranch hand. They didn't keep more than a pound of nails around at any one time either.

"Nope, none yet. Got several bagging up, though."

"Good. How's things with the house? Coming along?"

"Yep, it's coming." He'd change the subject. "How's Faith? And my sweetie-pie, little Dawn? And the new baby?"

Luke's grin about split his face. "A houseful. Kind of why I volunteered to ride into town. I needed a moment of peace. Gettin' up three times a night to feed Holly is taking a toll on Faith. She's tuckered all the time. Dawn thinks Holly is the cat's meow. Colton is pretty smitten, too, except he complains he's not going to have any eardrums left by the time he's ten." Luke shook his head with pride. "That boy is special. It's amazing how he keeps a protective watch on his sisters at all times."

Chance liked thinking he might be in Luke's shoes someday soon. He longed for roots, a wife, children of his own. What would holding his own baby feel like? He was ready. Girl or boy, didn't matter. If his family turned out anything like Luke's, he'd be one darn lucky man.

"Is that the plan you have there?" Luke asked. "Let me have a look."

Chance unrolled the sketch and held the paper open against the rail.

Luke leaned forward and studied the drawing for several long seconds. He whistled. "I like it, Chance. Looks like you'll have room to grow."

Chance felt his face go hot.

"It's larger than I expected."

"I expect you're right."

Chance hadn't yet shared his involvement with the mail-order brides agency and his plan to marry Evie Davenport. He didn't intend to, either. That was his and Evie's business, no one else's. There would be plenty of jokes and ribbing to go around when she arrived, he was sure.

Actually, he'd been skeptical when he'd first read the ad, and even after the idea took hold and he'd sent his first post. But then a letter arrived for him, written by a girl who didn't even know him. He'd read the missive most every night since, and the other two letters, too. If she was willing to take a gamble on him, a man she'd never met before, he'd sure take one on her. He'd care for her, protect her, and shield her from the razzing that was certain to come.

Chance rolled the drawing up and crossed his arms. "What's brought you into town?" He looked around. "Matt and Mark with you?"

"No, but Francis is. We came to pick up some doohickey for Faith at the store. You know how sensitive women are. Pays to stay on their sweet side." He lifted a brow and smiled.

"Frankly, no, I don't know." *Not yet. But I will.*

Luke had the decency to look sheepish. "Oh, yeah, right."

Chance let his friend off the hook with a smile. Years ago Chance had been sweet on Faith, Luke's wife and mother to his new baby daughter and two step-children. Chance had fallen hard from the moment he'd seen her step from the back of her rickety old wagon surrounded by all the cowhands. He'd hoped to woo her heart—had even risked breaking his neck trying to impress her on a loco-headed bronco. The sting of that day still had the ability to prick his pride. He could almost smile about the scene now, Faith fawning over him on the ground while Luke looked on, jealousy nearly turning his skin green.

Chance had always been reticent around women, and after Faith chose Luke over him, that reticence had only grown stronger. His shyness was a handicap. He'd all but given up hope of finding a wife until he'd seen the advertisement from the mail-order brides agency in the *Y Knot Sunday Herald*.

Even now, just the thought of all the talking he'd have to do to court a woman made his palms sweat and his heart thud against his ribs. He just wasn't much of a talker. And without words, attracting a woman was difficult—they liked to chatter about as much as they liked to shop. As soon as Evie arrived, he'd have plenty of talking to do. She'd expect conversation, and he didn't want her to think she was marrying a dolt. A cold, clammy anxiety wrapped around him like a damp blanket.

Luke's brows drew down in concern. "Hey, man, you feeling all right? Looks like you just saw a ghost."

Chance studied Luke's face. Maybe he should confide in his longtime friend about Evie. Maybe he wasn't thinking straight. Possibly he should call this whole thing off before he got in deeper, unable to pull his way out of the quicksand. He shook the notion out of his head and straightened his spine.

Luke stepped closer, an alarmed look in his eyes. "Chance? Say something."

"Hey, Chance," Francis said in greeting, joining the two. The young man's messy brown hair was in need of a trim. He stuck out his hand and the two shook.

Chance pulled himself back together. "Francis, how's life treating you out at the Heart of the Mountains?" It was good to see Francis. He'd shared the bunkhouse with him for years. He had always liked the boy and thought of him as a younger brother.

"Good, good."

"Yeah, what else *can* you say with your boss standing right here?" Chance laughed and winked at Luke. "Anytime you want a change, you have a job with me."

Francis's cheeks reddened as he looked back and forth between the men. He'd grown tall in the last year and stood almost eye to eye with them.

"Don't you go stealing my help, you sneaky Texan. Can't trust you as far as I can throw you."

"By the way, Francis," Chance said, cocking a brow. "Seen Charity lately?"

Francis sighed. "You know full well Charity only has eyes for Brandon Crawford. I wish you all would just lay off!"

Chance held up his hands as if fending off an attack. "All right, all right, I was just teasing."

Francis shook his head. "And don't I know it. Everyone still thinks of me as a snot-nosed kid."

"You're right," Chance replied. "I keep forgetting you're not a boy anymore. You won't hear any teasing out of me in the future." *I best remember what goes around, comes around.*

"Well, you might from me," Luke said with a chuckle. "Did Mr. Lichtenstein have that thingamabob Faith ordered?" he asked, looking at Francis.

Francis unwrapped the brown paper he carried. "You mean this?" He carefully held up a soft pink chemise decorated with tiny pink-and-blue flowers and a white silken ribbon.

"Exactly." Luke quickly took the unmentionable from the youth's hands and wrapped it back up. His face flushed. "Don't you dare tell her you picked it up." His voice brooked no argument.

Chance gave a long, low whistle. "Can I see that again?"

"No." Luke looked down to the sheriff's office. "Have you seen Brandon around? Thought I'd stop by and chew the fat as long as I'm in town."

Chance doffed his hat to Mrs. Harper as she walked by. Luke and Francis followed suit. "No, he told me this morning he's taking some time off. Rode out, but didn't say where he was going."

"That's strange," Luke said. "I wonder why he didn't say anything to me about it. Could be he's sore about Charity going off to that Miss Manners school down in Denver. I don't think he was too happy about it."

Chance shrugged. "Who knows," he said nonchalantly. "Those two don't know if they're coming or going half the time. I can't keep track."

Luke gathered his reins and stepped into the street. "Lucky said for me to tell you, if I saw you, not to be such a stranger. Just because you have your own spread doesn't mean you can't come out to visit us now and then."

"Tell him I will."

Luke mounted up and spun his horse around, then quickly turned back. "Oh, I almost forgot." He rode forward with a grin that said he'd just thought of something incredibly funny.

Francis, still standing with Chance, looked up at Luke curiously.

"Remember that advertisement in the paper awhile back, the one for the mail-order brides?" Luke asked, leaning forward with his palms on the saddle horn. "Seems someone from Y Knot actually answered it. Faith heard the news from a friend who heard it from a friend who heard it from Mr. Simpson, the postmaster. You know how forgetful he is. Well, he can't remember who sent the post but said he definitely saw a letter go out, maybe even a couple. I wonder who the heck it is?"

Chance removed his hat and fiddled with the brim. "That's quite the news," he said casually, running the side of his hand down the crease, then pulling the Stetson on firmly. "A mail-order bride, you say?"

Smile crinkles formed at the corners of Luke's eyes, and he laughed. "Yep, that's exactly what I said. Looks like a wedding is in the works."

Chapter Three

Evie entered the dormitory after a long day of work. She carried a large pitcher of water filled to the brim, being careful not to spill any on the hardwood floor. The large room, converted from the ballroom, faced west, letting in golden streams of evening light. Three beds graced opposite sidewalls. Each had its own private washstand with amenities. A coffee-colored trunk with a silver lock sat at the foot of each, large enough to hold some personal belongings. The carved walnut ceiling was the room's crowning glory.

Evie sighed. The lovely room was reserved for the girls who could pay a bit more. She would miss the grandeur when she left, but not enough to want to stay. This evening the brides-to-be were in the parlor, enjoying tea as they practiced writing poetry. Laughter floated up the stairs as Evie went about filling the girls' individual water jars. Finished, she turned down the coverlets.

"Evie."

Evie turned. Trudy stood in the center of the tall, double-door entry, warming her with a thoughtful gaze. The girl hurried forward. "I can't believe you're still working."

"Actually, I'm finished for the day." She stretched her weary back muscles.

"Well, thank goodness! I think Prudence should have to fill the water pitchers." They both giggled.

"I've wanted to talk, but we never seem to have the chance." Trudy sat on the side of her bed and patted the spot next to her. "Sit for a moment. I have a niggling headache tonight and Mrs. Seymour said I could retire early. I'll not be missed."

Evie did as Trudy requested and sank into the mattress. It was softer than the beds in the attic dormitory on the floor above, where three of the other girls lived. Evie herself had a small private room on the first floor next to Dona's, the cook. Trudy took Evie's hands into her own. "Can I tell you something?"

Evie nodded.

"I'm a tad nervous about being a bride. I can't admit that to anyone else but you. You're so kind to everyone, and thoughtful. You always have something nice to say. I appreciate that, more than you could know." She gave Evie's hands a little squeeze. "I feel close to you."

Evie warmed under the compliment.

"I've wanted to do this for so long, start my life, see the world. It's been my dream to go west and marry a wonderful, caring man, but..."

Trudy looked so vulnerable sitting there, her expressive blue eyes searching her own. "I'm not supposed to say anything yet, but"—she leaned forward and lowered her voice—"Mrs. Seymour has already found a match for me. I've known ever since I arrived but wasn't able to say anything until she checked out my domestic abilities. I guess I passed the test."

Evie gasped. "With flying colors, I'm sure. Who is he?"

"A farmer in Sweetwater Springs, Montana. Mrs. Seymour is enthusiastic—she says she's never had such a flawless match. From what Seth Flanigan said he wanted in his initial letter, I'll make him a picture-perfect wife. Apparently, that's never happened at the agency before. There's usually a little give and take. We're waiting for his reply," she finished solemnly.

An emotion-filled moment passed between them. "That's wonderful news, Trudy. I'm so happy for you."

Trudy smiled.

Evie tipped her head. "Isn't that why you're here?"

"Yes, I know. I can't wait to travel west, especially to Montana. I've dreamed about the mountains and nature for as long as I can remember. It's as if my spirit has always known I'd end up there. I like the idea of the wilderness too. Going to places no one else has ever seen." She sighed. "Actually, things are turning out better than I'd ever imagined. But…there is one thing that is making me sad."

Evie couldn't imagine anything that would trouble a no-nonsense go-getter like Trudy. *What courage and confidence!* "What is it?"

"After I leave I'll be worrying about *you*. Working your life away. Never finding a husband of your own. Evie, is this what you want?"

A lump rose in Evie's throat. She shook her head.

"Do you have family? Somewhere else you can go?"

"No," Evie whispered. "My mother worked here for Mrs. Seymour and the Colonel for as long as I can remember. They let her bring me here too, even though…" It was as if Trudy knew what she was going to say. The empathy in her eyes pulled at Evie's heart. "Even though I didn't have a father. And my mother wasn't a widow."

"Is that why you've not tried for a husband through the agency? You're beautiful and smart. I wondered why."

Evie nodded. "I'm not…you know…one of those girls of good moral standing." Several seconds passed before Trudy seemed to catch her meaning.

"That's preposterous! Of course you are. You should have a chance, too. Your morals are perfectly respectable. Your parentage shouldn't matter. I'm going to speak with the matron tomorrow, try to change her mind. You have so much to offer a man. Whoever he is, he'd be lucky to have a wife like you." Trudy bolted to her feet. "On second thought, I'll never be able to sleep a wink if I don't talk to her right now."

Panicked, Evie shot up off the bed and snatched the back of Trudy's gray chiffon sash, halting her in her tracks. "Please, Trudy, you mustn't do that."

When Trudy turned, the fire in her eyes was gone, replaced with puzzlement. "Why? Let me help you while I still can."

Excitement for the secret she was about to share bubbled up, heating Evie's skin. She couldn't stop a smile from playing with her lips.

"What?" Trudy's eyebrows lifted in curiosity. "Tell me."

"I've taken *matters* into my *own* hands."

It was Trudy's turn to gasp. "What?" They sank back down onto the side of the bed, face-to-face.

"You have to promise not to tell a soul."

"Of course."

"One day, when I went to our mail drop to collect the mail, the strangest feeling came over me. Like something significant was about to happen. Gathering the letters, I glanced down. There were three. All looked to be from prospective grooms. I studied each, but one kept pulling my gaze like a magnet. Before I knew what I was about, I dropped that specific post into my apron pocket. Later that evening, after my work was done and everyone was asleep, I opened it. I must have read the missive fifty times. He was so shy, so sweet. I knew I could be the perfect wife to him. So, I answered it. I'm going to be a mail-order bride myself."

"Oh…my…stars!" Trudy clamped her hand over her mouth for several seconds. "What's his name? What's he like? Tell me everything you know." Trudy said quickly without taking a breath. "I'm *so* proud of you."

"Chance Holcomb." Just saying his name brought a rush of heat to Evie's face. She giggled. "He has a ranch with a new house, in Montana, too. Just like you. He's tall and has brown, sandy-colored hair, and is incredibly handsome."

"Did he say *that*?"

Evie laughed. "No. But it's true—I just know it."

"How old is he?"

"Twenty-seven."

"You said Montana. What's the town called?"

"Y Knot."

"Why not what?"

"No. The *town* is Y Knot. With the letter Y."

They both burst out laughing, flopping backward onto the bed. Trudy clamped her hand over Evie's mouth. "Shhh, Mrs. Seymour will hear us."

Trudy grew serious. "When are you going to tell her?"

"I can't. I wouldn't know what to say. I can't imagine how upset she'll be, me going behind her back. Everything's been going around and around in my head for days. All that really matters is that Chance is expecting me. Has asked me to be his wife. If I speak with her, she may stop me from going."

"When?"

"Three days. On my day off. I'm leaving behind a portion of my earnings, enough to pay for the matchmaking fee and room and board if Mrs. Seymour *had* actually matched Chance up with me, or someone else. Still"—she paused and looked down—"I feel unscrupulous not being truthful with her. It's not the way I'd like to say good-bye."

She fiddled with her apron, which was lightly soiled from the day's work.

"I hope the money will also compensate for me not giving notice. *Not being truthful.* I've spoken with a friend of mine who recently lost her job when her employer passed on. She's promised to apply."

"You're being too hard on yourself, Evie."

"I don't like sneaking off without explaining, but I don't know what else to do. I can't imagine what her reaction will be."

Trudy shook her head. "You don't want to start your new life out with a falsehood. That would be bad luck."

"I don't have any other choice. What's done is done."

The sound of approaching voices propelled Evie up off the bed. She picked up the empty water pitcher to go.

"Wait." Trudy went to her trunk and hastily rummaged through. "Here." She brought out a small, beautifully cross-stitched handkerchief. "This was my mother's. Carry it at your wedding. Something borrowed, something blue. But do mail the keepsake back to me—to my father's home—as soon as you've wed so I can take it to Montana and carry it at my wedding. And send me a letter, too, telling me all about Chance and your home and—everything else. If we keep writing back and forth our friendship will never die."

Evie sucked in a breath. "A gift from a mother is much too precious to lend, even for a short time." When Trudy wouldn't take the memento back, Evie glanced down. Blue stitches on white. *Love Never Fails.* That was all. But the sentiment was more than enough to release the storm of tears she'd been holding back all day.

Chapter Four

The last of the afternoon sun glimmered through the aspen leaves as a gentle breeze eased across the land and ruffled Chance's hair. The house was a bit further along, but not much. Mr. Lichtenstein had found ten pounds of nails from somewhere, making it possible to get the outside walls up and most of the interior studs set. The structure was like a big box with a front porch and a magnificent view of the night sky. Chance was actually going to miss the sight when the roof went on.

Sweeping sawdust and wood shavings into the middle of the room, he let his mind wander. He enjoyed every aspect of construction, from digging the foundation to cleaning up each night. The house had taken on a life of its own. At some point in time, his bride would make the place warm and welcoming. Right now, though, the dwelling's personality was somewhat somber, a sort of wait and see.

Bending over, he reached for a nail bent squarely at the tip, then tossed the object into a tin can. He'd learned the hard way how precious even one nail could be. No shame in pounding a used one straight to use again. Ambling to the front door opening, he stopped and leaned on the broom handle. The wide-open acreage was like a balm to his soul.

The homestead faced east. Directly across was an enormous old oak that gave the front of the house a vestige of shade. Two hitching posts on either side of the porch dressed up the plainness of the yard, then the land rolled out into a rambling pasture, where his small herd of beef—each wearing his big *H*, little dangling *C* brand, for Holcomb Cattle—now grazed. Around behind and a distance away on a raised plateau was the holding tank for water pumped from the windmill that stood beside the barn. Last year, the well and water system were the first things he'd put in. His father would be proud to see what he'd accomplished almost single-handedly.

He'd been delighted when a heifer was born last night, a new addition to his herd. The spindly little creature now slept peacefully, curled in the grass, while her mama grazed by her side. The wagon trail into Y Knot curved from the west and rolled up between sparsely placed trees to the homestead. On the left-hand side of the yard was the barn, the structure he'd felt most important to finish before the fall, and before the snows hit. Then came a small smoke shack and outhouse. All he needed to complete this picture was a wife. *Evie.*

At that thought, he shifted uneasily. Five days had passed since he'd sent the post with Evie's fares. One for the train from St. Louis to Waterloo, and the second for the Wells Fargo stage from Waterloo on to Y Knot. Maybe he should have insisted on traveling to Missouri to fetch her himself. Make sure she made the trip safely. He'd offered and she'd declined.

Still, worry preyed on his mind. He'd sent one last quick note to explain one more time how far Y Knot was from any big town. Then, on a sentimental whim, something had taken hold of his senses and he'd stuck a tiny buttercup into the envelope, just something to make her smile. He shook his head. He'd turned into a sap.

It was strange. He wanted to protect her, love her, watch her marvel as the geese flew overhead on their way to warmer grounds. Was loving someone you hadn't even met possible? His heart said yes, at least with respect to him and Evie Davenport. Evie Holcomb, he corrected in his mind. He wanted to open up to her completely. Hold nothing back. Still, a tiny voice in his head whispered for him to go slow. Test the waters. Things weren't always what they seemed. The memory of his mother kissing him good-bye, breaking his heart, was a reminder he best never forget. He scrubbed a hand over his face, and looked into the sky.

Dexter, his black-and-white border collie, bolted out from the aspen grove, his tail tucked tightly between his legs as he ran hell-bent for the house. As he approached, the scent of skunk permeated the air. "Down!" Chance called when the dog was within thirty feet. "Don't you dare come one step closer."

Dexter dropped to the ground and woefully placed his nose between his two outstretched legs. A pitiful moan drifted over to Chance, along with a stink that would make a sailor cringe.

Chance let the broom drop to the floor with a sharp rap and strode across the porch, down three steps, and over to the animal. "I don't feel a bit sorry for you. You *know* better than to chase that cantankerous critter. This is the fourth time this year he's sprayed you."

He and Dexter had been a team for almost three years. Dexter was a darned good dog, too, great at herding, knew all his commands. Chance couldn't run the ranch without him. Now though, Dexter looked as if he were trying to disappear into thin air. What could he do? Skunk lasted a long time. What a nice welcoming gift for Evie.

The dog kept his head down, ashamed.

"Evie's scheduled to arrive on the stage—*tomorrow*."

A pitiful sound vibrated from the dog's throat.

Chance chuckled, unable to stay mad at his friend for long. "All right. I forgive you. Let's get you washed up as best we can."

Evie clutched the windowsill of the rocking Wells Fargo stagecoach as mile after mile of rugged land passed before her eyes. Patches of dense forest, flat open grasslands, mysterious-looking mountains far off on the horizon put a shiver in her heart.

Her stomach churned. The inside of the coach was musty and warm, and the motion made her tummy tilt and sour. If she never stepped foot inside another coach after this trip, she would be happy. This was not how she envisioned meeting her betrothed—with droopy hair, a sheen on her forehead and nose, and in need of a good scrub.

Sighing, she glanced at the small book Mrs. Seymour had given her at Christmas—*The Ladies' Book of Etiquette, and Manual of Politeness for the Use of the Lady in Polite Society* by Florence Hartley.

She opened to the first page.

1. Conversation is an art. A lady learns to sympathize while listening attentively. It is ill-bred to interrupt. Use a clear, distinct voice. Read and listen wherever there is an opportunity and store away knowledge for stimulating topics to speak about later. Affectation is vulgar. Keep purity, honesty, and charity in mind at all times.

2. The way to make yourself pleasing to others is to care for them. Truly, from the heart. Make sacrifices. Show them they are important to you. Affectionate, tender looks. Tiny acts of kindness. Give others the preference at every occasion.

Evie closed her eyes, recalling the cool, misty morning three days ago when she'd left St. Louis for good. She'd donned her most serviceable brown muslin dress, with a fitted bodice and drop waist, keeping the yellow serge for Sundays and visiting, and the blue hand-me-down velvet for her wedding. She'd brought along her black uniform, too. With the pretty, detachable crocheted collar and cuffs Trudy had given her, Evie was sure the black skirt and shirtwaist would come in handy on many occasions.

Also, after much heartfelt soul-searching about space, she'd packed both her aprons, the ruffled for company and the serviceable for her everyday chores. If she wore them with something other than her black skirt and shirtwaist, no one would know they'd been part of her maid's uniform. She had so few articles of clothing, leaving something so useful behind would be a mistake. At the last second, she'd stuffed her feather duster into her carpetbag, too. She'd had the implement for years, and something about leaving it behind just didn't feel right.

That morning, she'd quietly snuck out the side door of the house to start her new life. Alone in the early light, she'd taken one last look at the large red-and-white Victorian that had been the only home she'd ever known. She'd been born there, and her mother had died there, and was buried in the cemetery down the street.

A squeeze of emotion gripped her heart as she had struggled to memorize the little details that made the house special. The tall, round turret that always made her think of

Rapunzel, locked away. The climbing yellow roses blooming on the trellis above the parlor window. The gingerbread trim. *Home.* But no longer. She was on her way to a new life.

With a bit of a heavy heart, Evie wiped her forehead with her every-day handkerchief.

"Get used to it."

Evie looked up. The woman she'd been traveling with hadn't spoken more than ten words since they'd boarded. Evie smiled, grateful for a distraction. "Get used to what?"

The woman looked to be in her thirties. Her dainty nose had just the perfect scoop and her fingers were slender and elegant, lovely to watch. Golden locks, when not done up as they were now, must reach all the way to her derriere. She wore a beautiful red satin gown and a string of red stones about her slim neck. Her smile was impish, but her blue eyes were what caught and held Evie's attention whenever she'd looked her way. Evie fought the niggle of envy warming her skin.

"Being dirty. This is the West, sugar. We're not in St. Louis anymore."

Evie sat forward, anxious to speak of her old home. When she wasn't sick with excitement and fear over finally meeting Chance, she was brokenhearted from homesickness. This was the first time she'd ever been out of the city. "You're from St. Louis too?"

The woman shrugged. "St. Louis, San Francisco, Boston. I've traveled the world."

"How exciting! Have you been to France?" Evie's mother had been part French and had shared many wonderful stories about Evie's grandparents before they came to America.

"Well, no. Not France. But lots of other places."

"Are you going to Y Knot?"

She nodded.

Why was a beautiful—Evie surreptitiously glanced at her ring finger—single woman like her going to a small, rugged, hole-in-the-wall like Y Knot? Maybe she was a mail-order bride, too. Mail-Order Brides of the West was not the only mail-order brides agency in the world. Evie noticed advertisements springing up more and more often. But she'd not ask anyone a personal question like that.

Her heart swelled. *My first friend.* "I'm Evie Davenport. Soon to be Mrs. Chance Holcomb. I'll be living in Y Knot, too."

The woman's softly colored eyebrow lifted, and Evie felt a tense undercurrent of some sort ripple through the coach. "Well, I'm pleased to make your acquaintance, soon-to-be Mrs. Chance Holcomb. I'm Fancy Aubrey."

Had she said something wrong? Evie wondered if she'd somehow inadvertently been rude.

Anxiety made Evie dab her forehead with the cloth in her hand. "I'm pleased to meet you, too. This is the first time I've traveled out of St. Louis. Knowing that you're from St. Louis is a great comfort to me. I hope we can be friends."

Fancy Aubrey smiled in her mystifying way and nodded. "Of course we'll be friends. Out here you'll find that women are outnumbered six to one. Any time spent in the company of the fairer sex is appreciated."

Evie squelched a sigh, not quite sure what Fancy meant by her last comment. "Yes, of course," she echoed. At the last rest stop, the driver had informed them they'd be reaching Y Knot at approximately three in the afternoon. She glanced at the tiny watch pinned to her bodice. They were almost there.

Chance pushed a hank of hair behind his ear, grimacing at his reflection as if he'd never seen himself before. He should've gotten a haircut. For the third time, he settled his Stetson on his head and turned his face from side to side.

He wrestled a stupid-looking smile onto his face. Gathered his wits.

"Hello, Evie, it's good to meet you. Meet you finally. Finally meet you?" He cleared his throat and tried again. "Miss Davenport, how was the trip? Miss Davenport? Evie? Hello."

Picking up a glass of water from the dresser top, he gulped down several swallows before replacing it.

This was harder than castrating the bull calves.

"Hello, Evie, thank you for agreeing to be my mail-order bride. My name is Chance Holcomb."

Disgusted with himself, he smacked the dresser in frustration. The half-full glass tottered and he grabbed it just as it fell. *Of course she knows my name, you idiot!*

Come on, simpleton. Get it right.

"Hello, Evie. The house I promised you isn't finished and you'll have to sleep in the snow."

He turned abruptly, paced tensely to the window and stared out, trying to see Y Knot through Evie's eyes. The town looked shabby. Why would a city girl choose to come to a place like this?

Turning again, he caught sight of his good coat laid out on the bed. He'd bathed and shaved—but forgotten the haircut. Oh, well. Nothing he could do about that now. The stage was due in fifteen minutes. Staying in the room for another moment wasn't an option. He needed to feel some air on his face to settle his stomach. Donning his jacket, he ran his palms down his trousers, then pulled open the door. The time had arrived.

At the bottom of the steps he met Francis in the entry of the hotel.

"Chance?"

Chance cleared his throat. "What're you doing here, Francis?"

"I could ask the same of you." Francis looked him up and down, fingering a small, paper-wrapped package he was holding. "Going somewhere?" He could see the boy had more questions, but was holding back.

"I'm here to—" they said at the same time.

Chance tried to smile, but it felt stilted. "You first."

"I need to ship this for the ranch. Forgot yesterday." He held out the box. "Putting it on the stage." He glanced at the wall-hanging clock. "Should be pulling in anytime."

"And you're in the hotel because…" If he could keep the kid talking, perhaps he'd forget to ask what he was doing here.

Francis's face went dark, the chip back on his shoulder. "It's a free country, Chance. I don't report to you."

"You're right." Chance opened the door and went out, followed by Francis. Time was short. He listened for the horses, the wheels, his heart smacking against his ribs.

The street was practically empty. Looked like he and Francis were the only ones interested in today's stage.

"Why are you all dressed up?"

Chance didn't have the opportunity to answer before the rumble of the stage drew their attention. A second later, a team of six horses, their necks and hips lathered white, their round, ruby-red nostrils surging for air, careened around the corner between the bank and assayer's office and approached

Cattlemen's Hotel at a lope. Dirt kicked up from the wheels, leaving a four-foot-wide track. All noise was drowned out as the conveyance headed their way.

Chapter Five

"Whoa, now," the driver called out. The man, weathered from years in the sun, drew back on the reins and worked the squeaky brake with his boot-clad foot. "Whoa there, boys and girls. Listen up. Come on down to a walk." He smiled and gave a quick wave to Chance and Francis as the coach rocked to a halt and dust kicked up all around.

Chance couldn't stop a smile from forming on his face. His belly settled and suddenly he was ready and eager to meet Evie. Who would've thought his feelings could flip-flop so fast.

When he stepped toward the stage door, Francis caught his arm.

"You!" The boy's huge eyes glistened with surprise. "Holy smokes saints alive! You're the one who sent for a mail-order bride!" He shook his head and then mumbled, "I can't believe it."

Chance pulled away from Francis and reached for the door, turning the warm metal handle.

"Chance?" a soft voice asked in a throaty purr as a woman wearing a tight red dress extended her hand.

Confusion rocked him as he helped her down.

"Evie?" Her powdered face and voluptuous figure were not what he'd been expecting. *Evie? His Evie was a high-class saloon girl?*

She batted her lashes. "Hello, darlin'."

Her seductive smile sent a jolt zipping through his body.

"Holy smokes saints alive," Francis whispered in awe from a foot behind him. "Holy smokes saints alive," he said again.

The woman's gaze zeroed in on Francis. "And what's *your* name, love?"

The boy gulped and started to shake. "Fra-Fra—"

"Chance?"

At the sweet sound, Chance swung around, relief flooding his heart. The voice and the sensibility of the letters he'd read so many times matched the young woman perched in the coach doorway, and he knew intuitively who she was.

Large, wonder-filled eyes searched his as he took in her silky, soft skin, small nose, and perfectly shaped lips. Her curly, honey-colored hair shone in the sunlight, though wisps here and there were albeit a bit frazzled from the arduous travel. Her slim figure almost looked girlish, instead of that of a young woman of twenty-two. Then she smiled and his heart took wings. A dimple transformed her cheek and her lashes dropped shyly over her eyes. He reached up, encircled her small waist with his hands, and set her gently on the ground. *My wife.*

"Evie," he said in a clear, practiced tone. "How was—" His voice wavered. He stopped. He gazed meaningfully into her expectant eyes. "Evie," he began again slowly. "You're more beautiful than a sunset bursting with rose-colored clouds or a December sky filled with twinkling stars." He blinked and prayed his face wasn't red. "I'm in awe."

The spontaneity felt good and natural, and he meant the words from his heart. *Wherever that came from, I hope there's more.* Her smile deepened and her cheeks tinged pink.

"Thank you," she said softly.

The other woman laughed and smoothed the side of her hair. "Well, darlin', that's one of the most romantic things I've ever heard a cowboy say. I'm impressed." She shook her head and patted Evie's arm. "I'm sorry, sugar, I just couldn't resist. You should've seen the look on his face." She turned to Chance and arched her brow in a challenge. "I'm Fancy Aubrey. Would it really be so terrible if I were your bride?" She waved her hand. "Never mind, don't answer that."

Chance tucked Evie's hand protectively into the crook of his arm and covered it with his own. The feel of his betrothed next to him was a heady experience, so much so he could almost forgive the saloon girl for jesting at the most important moment in his life. Whoever she was, he didn't appreciate her kind of humor. Francis stood gawking, his shocked gaze going from one woman to the other.

Across the street, Hayden Klinkner stepped out of the leather shop. His rival stopped, boldly staring at Evie as if she were a cup of cream to a starving tomcat. Chance stiffened and Evie looked up at him, then followed his gaze across the street. Klinkner's smile broadened and he touched the brim of his Stetson. Chance heard Evie's soft intake of breath. Hayden chuckled, turned, and walked away.

Before Chance could respond, the driver came around from the back of the stage and handed him a carpetbag. A muted clanking sounded within.

Evie smiled. "A gift from my dear friend back home."

"How about some help with these trunks?" the driver asked a still stunned-into-silence Francis. "They're back busters. Almost crippled me gettin' 'em up."

"I'll do it," Chance said. Taking hold of the handgrip, he climbed up the stage and went for the largest trunk, hefting it. A grunt almost slipped between his teeth. "Careful, Francis," he cautioned, muscling the large, blue-and-pink-papered chest down, trying not to bang the container around too much. Holy smokes saints alive, he thought, using Francis's favorite phrase. *What's she got in here, bricks, rocks, anvils? A few nails, if I'm lucky.*

Francis staggered back a step, the trunk teetering above his head. The driver jumped forward to help. "See what I mean? I ain't never seen the likes."

Without looking down, Chance sensed Evie's intense gaze. He wanted to make sure she knew just how strong he was. Quietly drawing in a breath, he attacked the second trunk with gusto, trying to keep a smile plastered on his face. Sweat broke out on his forehead. "Here she comes."

Francis and the driver received this one together. From the corner of his eye, he saw riders coming up the street. McCutcheons. Three of them. Before Chance could lower the last trunk to Francis, they reined up alongside.

"What's going on?" Matt, comfortable in the saddle, looked from face to face. "This some sort of get-together?"

Mark nodded. "Sure looks like it."

Luke sat without saying a word.

Chance's face and neck, already warm and red from the strenuous lifting, heated almost painfully. He glanced down at Evie, who was studying the brothers with curiosity. At that, a jolt of jealousy took hold of him, shredding his poise like a raccoon with a honeycomb.

"Here she comes, Francis." With every ounce of strength he had, Chance hefted the last trunk as if the contents were nothing but weightless feathers and, though his teeth nearly cracked from the bite of his clenched jaw, handed it down smoothly, then followed in its wake. Back on the hard-packed dirt, he straightened his rumpled coat and brushed the dust off his trousers. He was surprised Francis hadn't yet spilled the beans.

Fancy strolled over to Chance, sashaying as she went. He could tell she was performing for the newcomers to see. "Thank you so much," she cooed. "I appreciate your brawn." She looked at the driver. "You think you can get someone to take these inside the hotel?"

Chance gaped at Fancy. "They're yours?" He shook his head in disbelief. "Why didn't you say so?"

"You never asked." She winked and fluttered her fingers. Then she walked from the stage to the hotel, drawing all male eyes to her backside, and disappeared inside.

Chance looked over at Evie, who was standing quietly with her carpetbag sitting by her feet. Possibly she's having her things sent out later. Or maybe—being she's a city girl, she wants to make sure this life suits her before going to the trouble and expense if she changes her mind about marrying me. The thought hurt almost more than he could bear.

Luke dismounted, his brothers following suit. Reins in hand, they approached, hats off and clamped to their chests. Evie inched a tiny bit closer to Chance, and his heart swelled.

Relieved that they seemed to have figured out what was going on, and were going to treat Evie with the respect she deserved, he said, "Evie, I'd like you to meet my good friends, Matthew, Mark, and Luke McCutcheon. They own the Heart of the Mountains, the largest spread in the territory. That's Francis." He pointed to the boy. "He works for them."

The four nodded.

"Men, this is Evie Davenport from St. Louis, Missouri. She's made me a happy man by consenting to be my wife."

Luke smiled. "We're pleased to make your acquaintance, Miss Davenport. We wish you and Chance much happiness."

"Yes," Matt added.

Thank goodness they were on their best behavior. This wasn't going to be so bad, after all, if the introductions were any indication. Although, as soon as they had him alone, he was sure it would be a different story.

"When's the happy day?" Mark asked.

Evie looked up at him. "I don't know," she said softly.

Luke clamped his hand on Francis's shoulder. "Whenever, you let us know. The McCutcheon clan will be there." He jerked his head. "Let's go, men. We have work to do."

They turned to go.

"Francis," Chance called.

The boy turned back. Chance gestured to the package sitting on the boardwalk. "Aren't you forgetting something?"

Evie stood patiently as several young hotel workers brought in buckets of hot water for her bath. Chance stood conspicuously by the door, shifting his weight from leg to leg. The lads poured the water into the copper tub, the splashing sound inviting. She couldn't wait to be clean.

Finished, they left and returned with a cloth-covered screen, set the partition up for privacy, then hastened out the door leaving her and Chance alone.

"I can't thank you enough for your thoughtful gesture, Chance." She willed her voice not to wobble.

Chance was everything and more than she'd thought from his letters. He'd said he was tall, and he was. His tawny hair was thick and lush, making her lips tip up at their corners just thinking about running her fingers through it. What would he do if she sauntered over, as she'd seen Fancy Aubrey do today in front of the men, and kissed him?

He caught her look. His face flushed.

A warm feeling pulsed through her veins. She quickly looked away. "But you needn't have spent the money. The room and the bath must be costly. I could have waited until we got out to the ranch."

He dropped his gaze to the floor at her feet. "You must be completely tuckered out. You bathe and rest and I'll be back at eight o'clock. We'll have supper in the hotel."

His deep voice sent shivers up her spine. "That sounds lovely." She thought he had a hint of an accent, but she wasn't sure.

He took a step toward the door. His eyes darted to the screen, with the bathtub filled with hot water behind, and then back to her face. "Can I get you anything else?"

"No, thank you."

"Well, I'll just be going." Taking his hat, he backed toward the doorway, never taking his gaze from her face. He stepped out and quietly pulled it closed. "I'll be back at eight, Evie," he called through the door. His footsteps disappeared down the hall.

Chance was *her* man, her husband-to-be. The notion was difficult to believe! Closing her eyes, she thanked God that his letter had stood out to her the day the three posts had arrived. Blessings from above. The girls back in St. Louis used to talk about marrying a cowboy, handsome and rough. And she was really going to do it.

And soon, she hoped. He appeared to be a respected member of this community. What would he do if he found her out? That all she'd ever been was a maid, and a fatherless one at that. That she'd opened mail that didn't belong to her. Would he be disgusted, send her away?

Evie didn't want to think about that now. Not with a hot bath waiting and the promise of dining with him later tonight—by candlelight in the beautiful restaurant downstairs. Immediately after her bath, she would write her first letter to Trudy, and have the post ready to send with the hanky the moment after she and Chance were wed. Who knew when that would be? Did he want to wait a bit to get married? Or was he as anxious as she?

Chapter Six

Chance hurried down the boardwalk and dashed into the livery. He glanced into the stall where Boston, his horse, munched on some hay. After haltering the gelding, he grabbed up his saddle and saddle pad and finished tacking him up.

"What's your rush?" June Pittman asked. She leaned over the double stall door, smiling in amusement. The livery had been her father's and when he passed on, the short, mischief-eyed brunette with an uncanny way with words had inherited it. She ran the place as well as any man could.

"Things." He hadn't meant to sound so curt. He liked June. She'd swim a river for a friend, even during spring runoff. He'd checked with her last week for nails. No go. After meeting Evie today, he was in an even bigger rush to finish that darned house. There'd been no mistaking that look in her eyes when she took in the bathtub, then gazed at him invitingly. He didn't want to disappoint her for long.

"Like nails?"

Chance whipped around. "You know that's it. Did you find any?"

She laughed, then shook her head. "No. Just wanted to see your reaction." She climbed up on the stall divider and sat, gripping a post for support.

He shook his head in irritation, then led his horse out of the stall and mounted. "Mr. Lichtenstein said there was a possibility I might find some in Grassy Gulch," he said, thinking that with her bushy hair, June looked like a squirrel on a branch. "That old place Markson used to own has a new owner. Moved in last month. Being they haven't been to town yet, he hasn't had a chance to ask 'em. Has a hunch they could very well have what I need."

"A hunch." Her tone dropped off, disbelieving.

"Right now a hunch is better than nothing."

She shrugged. "That's a ways out. You coming back tonight, or going out to your place?"

Chance looked at the sky. He could be out there and back in two hours. Plenty of time. "I'll be back. Staying the night in town."

She gave him a funny look. "You're a strange one, Chance Holcomb. A man on a mission looking for nails." She laughed. "You better get moving."

At seven, Evie began to dress, taking extra care with each step. She picked up a jar of honey rose cream she'd bought in Waterloo before boarding the stagecoach. Scooping up a large dab, she worked the salve down her neck and over her arms and hands, all the while thinking of Chance and the evening to come. It smelled heavenly and other than the drop sapphire necklace she'd inherited from her mother when she'd died, was the finest thing she'd ever owned. Finished, she touched her fingertips together, marveling at how soft they felt.

She looked at her dresses in the wardrobe with dismay, trying to decide which to wear. She'd shaken and hung them as soon as Chance had left, in hopes the wrinkles would fall out by tonight. The beautiful sheets and doilies she'd taken such pride in ironing for Mrs. Seymour popped into her head. Each had to be perfectly pressed, not a wrinkle to be found. She'd need to learn to be a bit less particular from now on.

She couldn't wear the blue velvet because she wanted that to be a surprise for her and Chance's big day. She'd not wear black—he might think her morbid. That left her brown travel dress and the yellow serge.

"Yellow," she said at last. She held the garment up in the mirror. Tipping her head to one side, she brought the fabric snug to her waist. An unfamiliar feeling, as rich as warm butter cream frosting, moved through her veins and brought a tingle to her skin. Her heartbeat quickened. She looked at herself through her lashes. "I—look—*pretty*," she whispered, as if someone listening might scold her for her pridefulness.

Leaving the dress on the bed, and still in her shift, she ventured to her open second-story window to watch the people on the street. *Maybe I'll see Chance,* she thought with a thrill. The crisp air tickled her skin, bringing a smile to her lips. Her senses fairly hummed in anticipation of the coming meal. She missed him. Wanted to be with him this moment. She wondered where he'd gone.

The last vestiges of sunlight disappeared, taking with it the shadows and most of the pedestrians. A man came out of the sheriff's office and went along the boardwalk, lighting lamps on street posts. The lights, flickering in a row, looked romantic.

Y Knot was actually larger than she'd anticipated from Chance's letters, with a number of interesting businesses along the street. Several women had passed by, most older, in buggies or walking. A pair of cowboys galloped up the street and slid to a stop in front of the Hitching Post Saloon, the establishment directly across from the hotel. Tinkling notes from the saloon's piano had just started up, and several newly lit lamps made the interior of the establishment glow.

She wrapped her arms around herself in disbelief and wonder. *Montana.* She'd have to get used to the big, open sky, trees as tall as the St. Louis County Courthouse, and the cry of an eagle that could surprise her at any time. The way she felt tonight, thinking of Chance, her life, and the beautiful mountain setting, probably added much to the magical aura surrounding her.

When the clock chimed half past, she donned her dress with shaky hands, not wanting to keep Chance waiting. She brushed her hair to a high sheen, fashioning the mass into a French twist and securing it with several pins and a silver clip. The usual unruly wisps curled around her face and glistened in the light of her lamp. Carefully, she took her beloved necklace from the cloth pouch and fastened the clip behind her neck.

An unexpected wave of emotion rocked her, and she squeezed her eyes closed. "Oh, Mama," she whispered. "I wish you could meet my Chance. He's the most thoughtful man. Heaven has blessed me mightily."

Ready for the evening, she sat carefully in a chair at the desk, listening for the sound of his boots.

Well, the new people had some nails, all right, a whole lot of them too, but none to spare or lend to him. They didn't know what the word neighborly meant. After an hour of horse dealing, talking, then begging until he was blue in the face, Chance ended up paying twice the going rate for five measly pounds. He divided them in his saddlebags and headed back. That was when he felt his horse gimping. He walked into Pittman's on foot, leading his horse.

Startled, June jumped up from her small desk against the street-facing wall, dropping her book. "You're back? The evening grew so late I thought you'd changed your mind."

Chance was in no mood to chat. The time was eight forty-two and six seconds, and he still needed to clean up. His clothes, the good ones he'd worn to meet Evie at the stage, were soiled and smelly. "Can you take care of Boston for me, June? He's limping on his left forefront. I looked but couldn't find anything unusual. No nail or broken glass. Might just be a stone bruise."

"Sure thing." She took his reins and ran her hand over the horse's neck, then gave Chance a long look. "How long you been walking?"

"Since the three-mile mark."

Eight o'clock came and went. As did eight thirty, then quarter to nine. Evie's stomach growled, protesting its emptiness. Where was Chance? Had he been hurt, killed? Who would know? How could she get any help? Who were the ranchers she'd met today at the stage? Matthew, Mark, and Luke. What was their last name?

She fought back a sob, a bottomless pit of misery that rocked her soul. Was this some sort of mean joke? He'd sent for her, hadn't he? Paid the money. A man wouldn't take matrimony lightly, would he? Had Chance changed his mind after meeting her? Perhaps Fancy Aubrey was more to his liking.

At that thought, a sob did escape Evie's throat. The sound came up of its own accord, bringing with it every hurtful, mean-spirited thing she'd had to live through, smile at, or pretend didn't hurt.

Christmas, when she'd rushed into the parlor to see what all the giggling was about, only to have everyone stop and stare at her until she slowly backed out of the room. The summer picnic she couldn't attend because she had to get the house ready for a new girl. Her fright when the group of brides-to-be she was with at the farmers' market forgot about her and went off, leaving her to walk home alone in the dark through a bad part of the city. Pitying glances as she went about her day. Sometimes cruel words delivered straight to her face. Not always, or often, but enough to make her feel different.

There were many good times too, yes, especially with her new friend, Trudy. But now the good times were hard to recall.

What had she been thinking? Someone like Chance Holcomb could have anyone. Any number of beautiful girls to call his own. He wouldn't want a maid, especially an illegitimate one at that. A girl who couldn't cook a lick, without a dowry, nothing to bring into the union that was beneficial for him. Had she been a blind fool? While she was dreaming about her handsome cowboy husband-to-be, he'd made his escape while the getting was good.

Stiff from sitting like a statue for forty-five minutes in the light of one solitary lamp, Evie remained silent as her heart quietly broke into two pieces, then four, then too many to count. Her dreams evaporated. She felt embarrassed for the lie she'd been selling herself. What should she do now? She swiped a single tear with the back of her finger. How could—

Chapter Seven

A soft knock sounded. In her misery, Evie had missed his approaching footsteps. Rising, she went to her mirror in the dimly lit room. Her eyes were red. Her hair, although fixed just as lovely as before, looked shabby to her now.

The knock came again. "Evie?"

Insecurities, born of years of service to others, of never measuring up in her own eyes, kept her rooted to the spot.

"Evie, are you in there?"

"One moment, please." Heavens! She sounded like the frog that lived in the carp pond behind the house in St. Louis. She stepped over to the door with as much aplomb as she could muster. She took a deep breath and, for one split second, prayed to God. Prayed that Chance might still want to go forward with the wedding. That he wasn't here to call everything off. Then, resigned for whatever was to come, she pulled open the door.

"Evie," he said gently in the golden light of the hallway. His gaze captured hers. Wouldn't let go. He was so handsome, his eyes alight with—with what? Oh, she was an expert dreamer, proficient in creating a reality she desperately wanted to be true. She struggled to look away, to gather her thoughts.

"I'm sorry. I didn't mean to be so late." His slight Texas drawl wrapped around her like loving arms. He held his hat, and his hair was wet around his temples.

"Chance," she said softly as she struggled to smile. Fought for one cohesive thought in her fog-muddled mind.

Across the hall, the door opened and an older couple stepped out into the hallway. The woman was garbed for dinner in a pretty jade dress and the man wore a coat and tie.

"Why, Chance, good evening," the man said as he took the woman's elbow. Evie didn't miss the look of curiosity that passed between them.

"Hello, Mr. Klinkner, Mrs. Klinkner," Chance responded. Stepping back, he brought Evie into the hallway with a slight touch to her back. "I'd like you to meet Evie Davenport, from St. Louis." His eyes searched hers as if looking for something deep inside. Was he sorry he'd kept her waiting? "Mr. and Mrs. Klinkner own the lumber mill on the outskirts of town."

Evie dipped her head, a habit she had from working all those years as a maid. "Good evening," she replied in a small voice. She was intensely aware of Chance by her side as she returned the woman's smile. His gaze was doing strange things to her insides.

"Speaking of lumber," Mr. Klinkner said. "Shingles are ready whenever—"

Chance straightened. "Good," he replied quickly. "I'll see to them tomorrow."

"It's a pleasure to meet you, my dear," the motherly woman said to Evie. "You're so beautiful. That shade of yellow is just perfect for you. Brings out the color of your hair."

The kind words were almost Evie's undoing. She willed away the moisture burning her eyes. Such an extravagant compliment! How was she to respond? How she wished she could just disappear into the air. "Th-Thank you, ma'am."

The man chuckled. Lines crinkled softly around his eyes and mouth. "Come on, dear, let's leave these two lovebirds alone. Not so long ago, I remember you alight like that. There's no mistaking the feeling when it's there." He placed his hand on the small of her back. "Even now that I'm old and tottering, I feel young tonight on our fiftieth wedding anniversary. The years have flown by."

The woman giggled like a schoolgirl and swatted his arm. "We're not so old, Norman." Her face tinged pink and she dropped her eyes.

"Maybe not, but if I don't get something to eat soon, I just may expire right here in the hall. Come along before they close the kitchen." He nodded at Evie. "A pleasure to meet you."

They watched as the older couple walked away, Evie feeling conspicuous and nerves rattling her insides.

Chance cleared his throat, then put out his arm. "Shall we go? You must be plenty hungry by now."

Before eight o'clock she'd been ravenous, her tummy growling up a storm as she visualized all sorts of delicious fare. Once the hour grew late and Chance failed to show, however, her appetite faded, then disappeared completely. She was afraid she wouldn't be able to eat a single bite.

Still, she nodded, taking his arm. Butterflies swirled and danced in her stomach. She felt so small walking next to him. The hallway was narrow, squishing them together. Embarrassing silence ensued.

At the top of the stairs, Chance stopped and looked down into her face. "You look beautiful tonight, Evie. Even more beautiful than before, if that's possible."

Be confident, Trudy had told her. And if you get flustered, just pretend Chance is Ernie, the son of the gardener who used to come to the house twice a month to care for the shrubs and trim the trees. Ernie had been a friend of hers for years, and the two could chat for an hour and not run out of things to say. She'd try to imagine Chance was Ernie right now.

She ran her free hand down the side of her dress. "Thank you. That's kind of you to say." Her response seemed to satisfy for his eyes warmed, and then he smiled. They proceeded slowly down the stairs.

They entered the dining room through the lobby door. Succulent smells and glowing candlelight enveloped her senses. A short, stocky man in a tight black vest and greased-back hair greeted them. Five or six tables took up the main portion of the room, but in each corner was a cozy booth. The only other customers were the older couple they'd met in the hallway.

So far, so good, Chance thought. He waited as Evie got comfortable in the booth, smoothing her dress over the fabric-upholstered seat. When she'd opened the door to her room, he'd been flummoxed. Her finely made gown looked expensive. Around her neck hung a jewel, the likes of which he'd never seen before. *Why would she travel all the way to Montana for a second-rate rancher like me? One she'd never met. She could have married anyone.*

She fidgeted in the booth one last time, then looked up at him and smiled. The light from a half-burned candle in the center of the table made her hair shimmer and glint. He hung his hat on the peg at the end of the bench post. Swallowing, he took his own seat. Straightened. Looked across the table at her.

Thankfully, the waitress appeared immediately. When she saw Chance, Lenore Saffelberg's eyebrow lurched up. He hoped the quick-tongued woman wasn't going to make some silly remark about his clothes. Or why he was here. Or how a month ago his horse, after pulling free from the hitching rail, had almost run her down as she crossed the street. She loved reminding him of that. He didn't frequent the expensive hotel restaurant often. Actually, he'd only been here a time or two. Once when Luke announced Faith was expecting, and the other time when he brought Francis for his birthday last year. The food at the Hitching Post Saloon suited him just fine, or, if he was splurging, he'd patronize the Biscuit Barrel for their tasty pies and coffee.

"Good evening," Lenore said. She slid her curious gaze from him over to Evie. "Jackson said you were here. That you're celebrating a special occasion, with a woman, no less. I see he wasn't making the story up."

Best just ignore it. "Evenin', Lenore," he said, avoiding her statements altogether. "I ordered a bottle of champagne. It should be chilling in the back. Can you bring that out—*please*?"

She pursed her lips and left.

"You like champagne?" he asked when Lenore was out of earshot.

Evie nodded.

"Good. I hoped you weren't going to say no. For all I know you could be a teetotaler—which would be okay, too," he added quickly. "I'm not much of a drinker myself, but I do have a sip now and then—you know, on special occasions." *What about the Hitching Post on payday and Saturday nights, sometimes other nights, too. Waking up with a headache. Should I be honest? Would that bother her?*

She nodded again, this time a small smile playing on her lips. Was she having doubts? Second thoughts about marrying him? After his ride out to Grassy Gulch, he'd been almost an hour late to the hotel, and rumpled from the effort.

But more than that, maybe Y Knot wasn't to her liking. She looked like a city girl through and through, with her feminine hands and creamy, soft skin. He'd be surprised if she'd done more than a lick of hard work in her twenty-two years. What would she think when he took her out to the ranch? Probably faint right away when she found out it would be just the two of them. No housemaid, no ranch hand, just him, her, and Dexter—smelling like a skunk.

He swallowed and surprised himself by wishing for sharp-tongued Lenore to hurry back with the champagne. "I guess it's time we get to know each other a little," he said. The older couple was all the way on the other side of the room, but that didn't stop him from feeling conspicuous. The evening was warm for a spring night. Mr. Klinkner had taken off his coat. He wondered if he could follow suit.

"You're right, Chance."

"Actually, I have something important to tell you about the house. There's been a—"

Her face brightened and it seemed her reluctance to speak melted away as quick as a one-minute snow flurry. "Oh, Chance, I have something for you. I forgot when I got off the stage. It's just a little thing, but—" Her hand flew to her mouth. "I'm sorry. I interrupted you."

"That's all right. Please, go on." He hoped beyond hope she wasn't going to give him some expensive bauble he couldn't match. He didn't have *anything* for her. The jewel winking back at him every few moments from around her neck was reminder enough that they were from two different worlds.

"I saw this in a house goods store in Waterloo before I boarded the stage," she said, taking a small something from her purse. "I hope you like it."

Her hand wobbled. He felt like a heel. He should have gotten her a gift, too. All he'd thought about was the smooth gold band in his pocket, wrapped up in a handkerchief.

As he took the wrapped gift, Lenore Saffelberg returned with the bottle of champagne and two crystal glasses. The waitress made a show of opening the bottle and pouring the sparkling wine.

The wrapped gift from Evie weighed heavy on his mind.

Finished, Lenore asked, "Would you like to order? It's getting late."

He nodded. "Sure."

"Your choices are steak with boiled new potatoes, steak with mashed potatoes, or steak with coleslaw. All three come with bread, butter, and bread pudding for dessert."

He glanced at Evie.

"I'll take the steak with mashed potatoes, please."

"How would you like it cooked? On-the-hoof red or dead broke?"

Evie sat for a second, looking at Lenore as if trying to figure out what she meant. "In between, please."

Lenore's eyes rolled to the ceiling. "Some folks just *have* to be different. Chance, how about you?"

Frowning, Chance reminded himself to speak later with Jackson about Lenore's behavior. He didn't care if she made him uncomfortable, but Evie was a different matter. "Steak with new potatoes, on the hoof."

Lenore nodded and hurried away.

He glanced up to find Evie watching him with clear, inquisitive eyes. What is she thinking? And why the heck didn't I think of a gift for her too?

Chapter Eight

"**B**efore I open this," Chance said, turning the small surprise over in his hands and smiling, "I'd like to make a toast." He picked up his glass and waited for her to do the same. "Here's to us. Evie and Chance."

Emotions played across her face, reminding him of clouds crossing the vast Montana sky.

"Yes," she finally said, smiling. "To us."

They touched glasses with a soft *tink*. He never took his eyes from hers.

She sipped and her eyes brightened. "This is wonderful."

The lightness of her voice reminded him of the lightning bugs he used to chase as a boy on hot, humid nights. He'd go out in his short pants and his ma and pa would sit on the porch, laughing as he ran around the barnyard, trying to capture one of the elusive critters in his hands. Those virtuous times had the power to heal his soul. Good times with lots of love.

He took another swallow and looked at Evie. How was one woman so darned beautiful? He should have told her more clearly how difficult a life in Montana would be. Days without company. Snowfall sometimes five feet deep, and cold enough to chill you to the bone. Or the sun, hot enough to drop you to your knees. No woman of her caliber would want to live here. Fear, the likes of which he hadn't felt since his mother walked out on him and his father when he was only six years old, overshadowed the happy moment.

"Chance?"

He'd slipped away, back to Amarillo. He struggled to focus on Evie. This should be a night of celebrations, not of sadness. "I'm sorry." He took in her worried eyes, the quaver in her voice. "I was just marveling at how beautiful you are. I'm not sure you're cut out for ranching. Have you ever been out of the city before?" *Better to find out now, than have her walk out this winter or, even worse, in a few years, leaving me and the babes.*

When a shadow crossed her eyes, Chance regretted he'd asked. "I'm just thinking of you."

"No, I've not been out of the city." She quickly took another sip of champagne, then set the glass down on the table.

Chance poured her a refill.

"Aren't you going to open the present I brought you?"

"Sure." He unwrapped the paper carefully, worried the gift might be fragile, and found that he was right. Chance uncovered a small pink-and-green porcelain plate bearing the expression Home Sweet Home, the words stacked one atop the other. A wire strung through a small hole at the top was meant for hanging. *I have no sweet home for Evie.*

He'd promised her a house, said the place would be done by the time she arrived.

"Do you like it, Chance?" Splashes of pink colored her cheeks, vestiges of the champagne, he was sure.

"I do. Thank you. I only wish I had something for you."

She smiled and reached out. "If you'd like, I'll keep it in my reticule until later." When she opened up her cloth purse again, a note card fluttered out and onto the floor. A large two-story Victorian home was etched in detail.

He picked it up to inspect. "Did you draw it?"

She nodded.

He was no expert, but the drawing was beautifully done. "What is it—besides a house, I mean?"

"Where I grew up in downtown St. Louis."

She's wealthy! Used to living in luxury. Montana living will be an unwelcome shock to her system.

"Your home?" he heard himself saying.

She looked at him for the longest time. Her brows drew down slightly before she nodded. "The only place I've ever lived."

Lenore Saffelberg was back with two plates. After setting them down, she rushed away and returned with a cloth-covered breadbasket and a pitcher of water. She promptly topped off their glasses. "Need anything else?"

Evie hadn't mentioned her financial situation in her letters. Only said her mother was dead, and he assumed the same of her father. What had happened to the red-and-white Victorian? Had they sold it? Questions raced in his head faster—

Lenore cleared her throat.

"That's all, thanks." His rumbling belly felt like a vast, empty ocean. He'd have to let his worries be and fill the void. Morning was the last time he'd eaten. The aroma of the pepper-covered steak made his mouth water, but the memory of that enormous house his bride-to-be had grown up in made his blood run cold.

Embarrassment vied with fear as Evie silently berated herself. She should have cleared up Chance's misconceptions about the Victorian! Hot tingles behind her eyes made her look away. How right Trudy had been! She should have told him the truth from the start. Shame filled her heart and she vowed she'd tell him everything when they knew each other better.

Fork and knife in hand, she cut into her steak. With the first bite of savory meat, Evie's appetite returned in force. The champagne warmed her blood more with each passing moment, and Chance, sitting in front of her with his charming smile, smoothed away her agitation.

Perhaps his lateness tonight didn't mean anything earth-shattering. Maybe he'd been working. Or got caught up in something important he couldn't put down. Whatever the reason, she didn't want to contemplate it now. This was *their* moment.

Chance chuckled and she glanced up quickly, realizing she'd been concentrating so hard she'd shut the whole world out.

"You're hungry," he said. "I know my gut is aching." He forked up a bite. "This is good."

She nodded, and watched him chew. His eyes fairly twinkled, making him a mixture of roughened cowboy and small boy. He was trying so hard to be polite, and he was succeeding. She was glad he wasn't some snobby, highfalutin businessman. She much preferred open and honest to guarded and calculating. Yes, he suited her just fine.

Chance swallowed and wiped his mouth with the white cloth napkin. "I haven't learned much about you, Evie, since we sat down. I intend to fix that right now. What's your favorite color?"

She looked off for a moment. "Blue."

To match your fine-looking eyes, he thought with an inner smile. "Good, we're finally getting somewhere. Favorite song?"

Again, sadness. He wondered where it came from.

"'Tell Him I Love Him Yet.' It's a song my mama used to sing to me."

"I'm not familiar."

"I'll recite the first stanza, if you'd like."

He nodded.

"'Tell him I love him yet, as in that joyous time. Tell him I ne'er forget; though memory now be crime. Tell him when fades the light upon the earth and sea, I dream of him by night, he must not dream of me.'" A moment passed. She sipped from her glass.

Deeply moved, he just sat there. There was no mistaking that song meant a great deal to her, and at this moment he sensed her heart suffered from some kind of loss. He wanted to lighten the mood, do something, but he didn't know what. "Mine is 'The Flag of Texas,' by Anthony F. Winnemore, about the battle of the Alamo—I won't be reciting it, though." He chuckled. "Have you always lived in St. Louis?"

"Yes, in the house I showed you."

"And your father?"

Her eyes darted away for a moment, and he was reminded of when Dexter was guilty of some infraction.

"I never knew my father. And speaking of him brings me anxiety. I don't know what he did for a living or even if he's still alive." Her voice faded to a hushed stillness. "How about you, Ernie—er, Chance?" she quickly corrected. Her cheeks blossomed to a dark shade of pink.

Hurt, Chance sat straighter, wiped his mouth with his napkin.

"I'm sorry!" she offered quickly. "That just slipped out. Ernie is a friend back home."

Of course she had a beau back home. How couldn't she with her fathomless sapphire eyes, graceful swan neck draped in jewels, and a dimple sweeter than cherry pie in spring. Right now, with his insecurities running amok, he wished she were on the plainer side, someone who wouldn't turn heads. Someone who'd be satisfied living out in the sticks, going weeks without seeing a neighbor, a woman who would stay around for life.

He waved a hand. "Perfectly all right. Please, go on."

"Before I was born, my mother was a teacher at a woman's university in St. Louis. She was kind, intelligent, loving. She passed on eight years ago. I miss her every single day."

Now they really were getting somewhere. Chance broke off a piece of bread and put it on Evie's plate. She smiled her thanks. "Your turn," she said.

"I was born and raised in Amarillo. My pa was a rancher too. We had a decent spread three day's ride west of town." *Ma just couldn't take that solitary life.*

"Do you have brothers and sisters?" she asked, taking a small sip from her champagne glass.

"One of each. An older brother and a younger sister. My sister died when she was three, and my brother rode out when he was fifteen. We never saw him again."

Evie's eyes went wide. "Why?"

"Don't know. I was just a kid. My pa never said."

"Chance, I'm sorry."

He waved off her concern. That was long ago, the hurts all but healed over. He did wonder about Nate, what happened to him, if he was still alive. He'd be thirty now. No way of finding someone when they don't want to be found.

Lenore was back. After inquiring, she picked up Chance's empty plate and Evie's half-eaten meal, then hurried off and returned with coffee cups. The Klinkners, now finished, got up and started in their direction. They stopped in front of their table.

"You're new in town, aren't you, young lady?" Mrs. Klinkner smiled at Evie. "I don't believe I've seen you around before. How I wish our son Hayden would find a nice girl like you."

Hayden Klinkner! One person Chance could live without. The two butted heads every time Chance went to the lumber mill for wood.

"Chance, you simply must bring Miss Davenport out for tea soon," Mrs. Klinkner said. "I'd love to hear about St. Louis and all the new fashion and eateries."

Not in this life, he thought. Hayden had a wild streak in him. A few years ago, there'd been rumor about him and a young wife over in Pine Grove. Seems she up and left one day, not telling anyone where she'd gone. He'd not dangle Evie in front of his nose like a piece of honey-covered chocolate.

"We live at the end of Creek Street across from the lumber mill. If Chance doesn't have time to bring you, you stop by yourself."

"Thank you, ma'am."

"Where do you live? In town? The homes on Lark's Foot Street?"

Evie looked to him in question.

"She'll be living with me. We're getting married."

Both the old folks' eyes went wide. "Married? When?"

He glanced at Evie to judge her reaction. This couple had helped him right into an uncomfortable topic he'd been wanting to broach. "Tomorrow?"

Evie's eyes widened.

If the town's not too remote for your liking, or I'm not too coarse for your genteel upbringing. "The circuit preacher will be coming in early. If it's still agreeable with you, Evie, I'd like to get that small detail taken care of." If she wanted to back out, this was her chance. "Now that you've seen Y Knot, and know how rough around the edges the town is, and now that you've met me too, do you still want to go through with it? Ranching is a hard life."

Mrs. Klinkner sighed, her eyes dancing. "How lovely! A mail-order bride?"

Evie nodded, an impish smile reappearing for the first since he'd left her to bathe. "I am. Chance and I just met today."

"Evie?" She still had not answered his question.

"Yes, Chance. That's agreeable with me. Nothing could change my mind."

Norman's eyes widened. "Now, *that's* romantic. Come on, dear. We've used up too much of these almost newlyweds' time already. And after that hearty dinner I can feel my eyes drooping. I'm about asleep already and I still have that long stairway to climb."

"You're not sleepy yet, are you? It's our anniversary."

"Maybe not," he responded. "But I may be soon."

They said their good-byes after Ina Klinkner made Evie promise to stop by someday soon.

"Did you mean it, Evie?" Chance asked. "Saying that tomorrow is agreeable with you?"

"I told you I'd marry you in my letter. Did you think I'd change my mind?"

"Guess I thought you being a city girl, maybe you would."

"Do you want me to?"

There it was again. Wariness. Like a skittish colt. "No, 'course not."

The smile that bloomed on her face was as welcome as a summer shower. "The little I've seen of Y Knot suits me just fine. Although, my experience has only been with the inside of my hotel room and now this dining room."

He reached across the table and took her hand in his. "We'll fix that tomorrow. Just as soon as we go to the church and say our vows. Afterward, I'll take you anywhere you want to go. We'll explore the town store by store, how's that?"

"I'd like that just fine. And then go out to the ranch?"

He swallowed. He needed a few more days and a whole lot of nails before the house would be ready to show. "Er, we'll see. But I also want you to know, I remember the stipulation from the bridal agency. About waiting a month. I'll honor that, Evie. You have nothing to worry from me."

She glanced away, and Chance figured she must be embarrassed.

Lenore was back with two bowls of bread pudding. "Your dessert."

Evie looked to him. "I'm much too excited to eat another bite."

"Me either." He couldn't believe his good fortune. She'd be the most beautiful bride the church in Y Knot had ever seen.

Lenore shook her head, then sighed. "Well, I *never.*"

Chapter Nine

Evie stepped out into the cool morning air with a firm hold on Chance's arm. A few people were out, going about their business. She snuck a glance at Chance, nerves pinging her insides. *Am I doing the right thing? What will he say when he finds out I stretched the truth?*

Well, there was no help for it now. After a leisurely morning spent in her room, enjoying a breakfast of tea and toast, they were finally headed for the church. She'd soon be Mrs. Chance Holcomb. The memory of Chance's face when she opened the door, wearing her blue velvet dress, which fit her figure perfectly, coaxed a smile and a happy giggle that chased away her fears. She was glad now that she'd worked her corset ties as far as they would go. She fingered the dainty white hanky with the blue letters she'd folded and pushed up inside her sleeve, taking strength from the sweet keepsake and Trudy.

"Something funny?" he asked, his quizzical expression punctuated with a smile.

"Just excited, I guess."

He patted her hand and looked down into her upturned face. "Good. Me, too. Just as soon as we're finished at the church, I'll show you the whole town. If you see anything special, I'll buy it for you."

"Thank you, Chance. I'm glad you brought that up. I need six bolts of fabric for some new clothes, a set of dishes to serve six, and a new silver-plated mirror and brush."

He stopped in his tracks.

She laughed again. "I'm just teasing you! I've brought with me all that I need."

He chuckled. "Well, you got me."

His deep voice, laced with happiness, was all she needed to confirm she was doing the right thing. As they walked several men rode by, their horses' hooves kicking up dust. A woman with a small child in tow glanced at her from across the street.

"This is the mercantile," Chance said as they passed a large general store. Huge plate glass windows on both sides of the Dutch door displayed all sorts of interesting things. Lichtenstein's Provisions, painted directly onto the glass, took up much of the room on both large panes.

"Looks like a nice selection."

Chance nodded. "It is." He mumbled something that sounded like, *Except for nails.* "If Mr. Lichtenstein doesn't have what you need, he'll do his best to order it for you." When she looked at him for verification, he smiled and said, "I'll introduce you later today."

An assortment of warm woolen scarves on the wall caught her attention, sparking an idea. "When's your birthday, Chance?"

When he didn't answer right away, she tapped him gently on his shoulder until he slowed and glanced into her eyes.

"Chance?"

A splash of color marked his cheeks. "Well, if you must know, it's in three weeks. The twenty-seventh."

Bouncing up and down on the tips of her toes, she couldn't contain her excitement.

"Yours?" he asked, smiling.

"October seventeenth. I'll be twenty-three." Mrs. Seymour had always had a festive birthday dinner for any of the brides-to-be. Evie would do the same for Chance, in their new home. All she needed to do was learn how to cook something good, like a rump roast with all the fixings or an Italian meatball and spaghetti dish. The aromas that filled the house whenever Dona had sautéed up the tomatoes and beef made her mouth water. Chance would think her a queen if she could do something like that. And, of course, a chocolate layer cake.

Her heart sank. Whom was she trying to fool? She'd never be able to accomplish all that in three short weeks. Chance would be so disappointed when he discovered her ineptness in the kitchen. Her smile wobbled, but she pushed the corners up. This was her wedding day. She wouldn't let anything spoil it.

"Come on. We don't want to be late," Chance said, coaxing her forward.

They passed an empty building with a front broken window, then started up an incline toward a small blue building constructed of milled boards. *That must be the church.* The structure was set back from the road. A good-sized open field extended out behind and several shade trees dotted the landscape. A small porch at the top of five steps would only hold a few people. A handful of hitching rails and water troughs were scattered about.

"Preacher's waiting." Chance's nod indicated a one-stall barn with a horse looking out. The empty buggy sat next to the fence. He looked down at her. "You getting tired? Your face is all flushed."

Tired? If he only knew. "Chance, you certainly don't know me very well, but then how could you?" She laughed softly. "Thank you for your concern. I can work all—" She stopped and quickly cleared her throat. "What I mean is I'm not a china doll to fuss over."

His expression said he didn't believe that for a moment. "Fine, then. This is your last opportunity, Evie. That's the preacher's horse and the preacher knows we're coming. I can tell you what a Montana winter is like, but until you've lived through one, nothing I say will prepare you for what's to come. It's tough, cold, and lonely. Once the snow hits, we'll be stuck out at the ranch for days, or even months."

Chance's brows arched over his eyes so earnestly, she was tempted to smooth away the worry wrinkle with her finger. She stopped and placed her hands on her hips. "Chance, you've tried to talk me out of our wedding now several times. I'm beginning to think you have cold feet, and just don't want to say so. Perhaps you're the one who needs to take a minute or two and make sure this is what you truly want."

The door to the chapel opened and a middle-aged man waved. He was medium in height and had thick brown hair. "Was wondering if you'd changed your mind, Chance. You're late."

Chance looked like the boy with his hand in the cookie jar. They started forward. "See what I mean," she whispered. "Others are noticing it too." She couldn't stop another round of happy laughter.

"You hush." He nudged her, and a flutter skittered up her spine.

On the church steps, Chance made the introductions. Reverend Kyle Crittlestick was a friendly, well-spoken man, and Evie liked him immediately. He and Chance talked on, catching up with Y Knot's latest news, while she quietly looked around. There were eight rows of pews and a roughly constructed podium in the front. Not much else inside besides a good-sized white cross and a wooden box that said For the Poor. Simple and sweet.

"I thought you knew, Chance," Preacher Crittlestick said. "You need a couple of witnesses, excluding me."

Chance turned and looked at her, dismay on his face. "Evie, I'm sorry. We need two people to stand up for us as witnesses."

Oh, no! She didn't want to wait. She struggled to draw a breath in her tight corset. What if he found out the truth? Or, maybe he had, and that was why he'd been giving her so many chances to back out. She didn't deserve such happiness, marrying a man as good as Chance. With her background and given the way she'd left poor Mrs. Seymour without a good-bye, she didn't merit him. But darned if she didn't want to marry him this moment.

She'd been dreaming about kissing Chance since reading his letters, and again when he'd circled her waist and helped her down from the stage. Visions of him filled her head, and thoughts of what lying in his arms would be like heated her skin. She'd tossed and turned until the early hours, imagining all sorts of exciting things. "Is there anyone in town you know, that wouldn't mind coming over for a minute?"

The preacher's brows lifted. "Not a bad idea if you don't want to wait till I'm back in three weeks, or whenever Sheriff Crawford returns."

Fluffy clouds dotted the sky as the midmorning sun winked through. The rays warmed Chance's back as he walked briskly down the sloping road, leaving Evie and the reverend behind. Whom could he find? He hadn't seen any of his friends in town this morning. He should have sent notice to the McCutcheons. Problem was, he hadn't been sure she was going to say yes. The Klinkners might still be in their room, but he hardly wanted to disturb them, being on their anniversary getaway and all. He chuckled. A getaway without leaving town.

He stopped on the corner, thinking. There were people he recognized everywhere, but no one he wanted to stand up for him and Evie. Jack Jones, Brandon's deputy, rode up to the sheriff's office and dismounted, but he liked Jones about as much as he liked warm eggplant on a cold day. Today was special. At that moment, Fancy Aubrey opened her second-story window at the Hitching Post Saloon and looked out. When she saw him her face brightened, and she waved. Nope. He wasn't going there. He smiled politely and nodded.

He took a few steps into the street and looked all the way down the block and across Half Hitch Street, at the livery. He liked June a lot. They'd been friends for as long as he'd been in town, but what would Evie think if he showed up with another woman on his arm?

"Out of the way, cowpoke! Or I'll run you down!"

He turned just in time to see Lucky wave, then wrangle the oversized buckboard he was driving to the side of the road. Francis sat beside the McCutcheons' bunkhouse cook.

"Didn't ya get the message from Luke?" Lucky grumbled loudly. "I told him ta tell ya ta get your backside out ta the ranch. Ain't seen as much as a hair on your head for a heck of a long time."

Blessed relief flooded him, and he couldn't stop a smile. There sat the answer to his prayer. "Lucky, you old goat, good to see you. Francis, you too."

Lucky jabbed Francis in the rib with a bony elbow. "Look out, kid, looks like he's up to no good. I've seen that gleam in his eyes before. Maybe that fancy mail-order bride up and left him already." Lucky glanced around, his eyes as sharp as a hawk's. "Where is she, anyway? Was hoping I'd get ta meet her."

Chance walked over and plunked his boot on a wheel spoke and tipped up his hat. "Just waiting on you, Lucky. Says she won't marry me until she meets the famous Lucky Langer from the Heart of the Mountains."

Lucky's mouth fell open. "What's this gibberish?"

"It's true. She's waiting on me as we speak, up at the church. Reverend Crittlestick is there, too. We need two witnesses and I'm hoping you and Francis will stand up for me and Evie right now."

Francis gaped. "Right this second? We need to get supplies at Lichtenstein's."

"Won't take but a minute." Chance stepped on the sideboard and grasped the back of the wagon seat. "My bride's a-waitin'! Turn this rig around."

Evie dared a look at the middle-aged man who followed Chance and Francis into the church, a distinct limp slowing his step. The cowboy held his hat in his hands and perspiration shined his forehead like a ripe apple. She remembered the boy from yesterday at the stage. Tall and lanky, he did everything but look in her direction.

Evie swallowed, heard Chance shifting his weight from foot to foot. Now that the time had arrived, her legs wobbled as if they were noodles straight from the pot. She didn't know if she would stay on her feet. When Chance left, she'd gone out in the field behind the church, picked a few wild buttercups and mountain bluebells, and put them together in a small bouquet. They weren't the Victorian's hearty roses, but to her, their sweet fragrance and delicate petals were all the more beautiful.

"Come on over here and line up," the reverend instructed. "You here, Lucky, and then Chance. Evie come in close. Now you, Francis."

"If we're all set," Reverend Crittlestick said, glancing around, "we'll begin. Dearly beloved, we are gathered here today in sight of God and man for the union of Chance Holcomb and Evelyn Davenport. If anyone present knows any reason this couple should not be bound in holy matrimony, speak up now or forever hold your peace."

Evie's mind raced. Perhaps she should have told Chance she was only a maid. That she'd taken his letters without permission and written to him on the sly. Was that grounds for divorce? Or the fact she'd never corrected his assumption about her cooking abilities, or the big house. Was she dooming her marriage by starting out with falsehoods, just as Trudy had told her not to? Oh, why hadn't she said something before it got to this?

She gave a little cough. "Uh, excuse me." Chance looked at her, askance. "May I speak with you for a quick moment in private?"

Chapter Ten

Chance's eyes widened with surprise. He glanced at Reverend Crittlestick. When a strained hush dropped over them all, Evie's heart shuddered. With a hand to her lower back, Chance escorted her to the far side of the room.

"What is it, Evie?"

She swallowed. Tried to keep the flowers in her hand from shaking the blossoms right off the stems. Behind Chance, the others were conspicuously looking in other directions except theirs. "It's just that there are a few things I meant to share with you last night at dinner," she whispered close to his ear, taking in his soapy, woodsy scent, his well-formed eyebrows. Warm tingles almost made her shiver. "As the evening went on and perhaps because of the champagne, I completely forgot. You asked me once—"

Chance held a warm finger to her lips. "Are you already married?" he asked, his voice earnest, low. Her heart shuddered.

"No."

"Have you killed anyone?"

She shook her head.

A smile played around his lips. "Are you wanted by the law?"

She glanced away, thinking. Was Mrs. Seymour trying to track her? Had she told the sheriff about her taking the—

"Evie!"

"There are things. I think I've misled you in believing—"

"Darlin', there're things I haven't told you yet either, just didn't know how to broach the subject. We can't know everything about each other by writing a few letters and having dinner once. I understand that. I hope you'll be as accepting when you learn my faults. Maybe I should explain myself to you. About the house and why we're staying—"

"No." Her forceful whisper stopped him short. "There isn't *anything* that I don't know yet that would stop me from marrying you, Chance."

He stared at her for a long second. "There isn't? Well—good." A smile reappeared on his face, and his eyes crinkled in the corners in the most appealing way. "As long as you're free to marry me, and you still want to, everything else is neither here nor there and will get worked out later. Agreed?"

"I guess." She forced a smile, but knew it must look silly. "I'm ready and willing."

Reverend Crittlestick's expression was uncertain when they angled back in between Lucky and Francis. "We all set? Questions answered?"

"Yes," they said in unison.

"As I said before," the preacher said, rushing the words out as if fearing another interruption, "we are gathered here today in the sight of God and man for the union of Chance Holcomb and Evelyn Davenport. No one has any objections, so we'll move right along." When he signaled for Chance to take Evie's hands, she turned and held out her bouquet to Francis.

Chance's fingers were warm, his hands large and roughened from work. Her heart shivered so fast she was sure she would swoon before she was able to say one word.

Her life at the agency came rushing back. The time since her mother's death, all the years wondering who her father was and why he'd abandoned them. Mrs. Seymour herself, trying, but never being able to make her feel truly wanted and loved.

She dared a peek from beneath her lashes. If there was a God in heaven, which she knew there was, how she wanted to believe the emotion she saw on Chance's face right now, trust the sparkle in his bottomless, dusty-green, wonderfully wise eyes. She didn't want this to be make-believe, one of the happily-ever-after stories she so often conjured up in her head. He was so handsome and earnest. He would be her husband in the next few moments, and the thought was heady, amazing. She was the luckiest girl in all of Montana.

"Do you, Chance Holcomb, take Evelyn Davenport to be your lawfully wedded wife? To have and to hold, from this day forward, for better and for worse, for richer and poorer, keeping only unto her, never forsaking her, until death do you part?"

"I do."

Chance never faltered or hesitated, his deep voice sending shivers up her back. She'd gulped in a huge breath at the word *wife* and clenched her eyes closed, expecting him to come to his senses and stop the ceremony.

Lucky chuckled softly. "Open your eyes, honey."

She did and looked around. They were all smiling.

She hardly heard what the preacher said next, but knew she was supposed to respond because they were all staring at her expectantly. "I do."

"Do you have a ring?"

Chance let go of one of her hands to dig in his pocket. He unwrapped a smooth gold band from a piece of cloth.

The reverend smiled. "Go ahead and slip it on."

The sight of the band warming her finger, her heart, was almost too much. She had no idea Chance had gotten her a wedding ring. One that resembled Mrs. Seymour's, Mrs. Klinkner's, or the wedding ring quilts she'd helped to sew. Her very own beautiful ring. Her heart swelled. Chance watched her so closely, she couldn't imagine what he was thinking.

"By the powers vested in me by the great territory of Montana, I happily pronounce you husband and wife. You may kiss the bride."

Chance took a small step forward and leaned toward her. His thumbs brushed across the backs of her hands as he placed a brief kiss on her lips.

Evie could hardly believe her dream had come true as his warm, dry lips brushed across hers, gentle, sweet. She thanked God in heaven she wasn't still back in St. Louis, destined to die an old maid without a home of her own, children on her knee, or this wonderful man to love.

But what about my lie, Lord? What would she do if Chance discovered the truth? She pushed the fear aside, wanting to enjoy her wedding. The deed was done, and she'd worry about the consequences later.

The ceremony was over. Chance was married to the prettiest filly this side of the Rockies. With her fancy blue dress, tiny waist, and golden done-up hair, Evie looked like a picture he'd once seen in a magazine. She sure brought a sparkle to Y Knot.

Lucky grasped Chance's hand, smiling like the town fool. "Sure glad ya included me and Francis in yer big day, boy," he said, wiping the tear welling in the corner of his eye. "Sure tickles my britches to be a witness fer the two of ya."

"Here, ma'am," Francis said, holding the buttercups and bluebells out in front of Evie. "Your flowers."

"Thank you," she replied.

Chance put his arm around her and pulled her to his side. "Thank you, Reverend. We appreciate—"

Evie gasped in fright.

Chance swung around, his hand reaching for the gun that wasn't strapped to his hip. He'd left his weapon in the hotel, being they were headed to the church and he didn't think it mannerly to be armed at his wedding.

Francis did draw his gun, though, and was searching for the culprit. Lucky looked around wildly when Evie let go another distressing cry. She flung her flowers to the floor and slid behind Chance, gripping him with the strength of Samson.

"What! What is it, Evie? What's wrong?"

Peeling her arms from around his middle, he turned around and gathered her quivering body into his arms. Her face was ashen. She tried to say something but only gulped for air, then squashed her face into his chest.

"Evie! Talk to me?" *Is the girl loco?*

"Sp-sp-*spider*," she finally got out, pointing at the array of blossoms scattered across the scuffed wooden planks.

It took a moment for him to find the black dot scampering toward the wall. "Why, that's just a harmless ol' daddy longlegs, Evie. He can't hurt you." She was shaking uncontrollably, her eyes fastened on the body no bigger than a tomato seed attached to eight long, wiry legs.

"Look." He bent over and scooped the spider up to show her, letting it crawl over the back of his hand and up his arm.

Evie swayed. Thankfully, a wide-eyed Francis reached out when her legs buckled, catching her before she hit the floor.

Lucky gave a long whistle, and Francis handed Chance his unconscious bride. "City girl, huh?" the cook asked, slowly shaking his head back and forth.

"Looks to be the case," Francis said. "Where's she from?"

Chance, distracted by holding Evie's limp body, managed to reply, "St. Louis."

Lucky scratched his head through his thinning brown-and-gray hair, his expression one of doubt. "You'll have yer work cut out fer ya," he said, his eyes still glued to the small woman in Chance's arms. "Montana's full of creepy critters." He put his hat on and started for the door. "Be sure ta bring her out ta the ranch soon. All the McCutcheon women have been atwitter since the men brought back the news of meetin' her." He cocked a brow. "That is, when she wakes up."

Chapter Eleven

Evie woke up by degrees. Motion rocked her, and a soft, cool breeze caressed her face. When she opened her eyes, she was gazing up at the underside of Chance's chin, held in his strong arms. The spider! She'd swooned. Heat born of embarrassment singed her insides and she thought she might die. *What must he think of me?* She pressed on Chance's chest.

He stopped walking and looked down. "You're awake," he said softly. "Do you think you can stand?"

Oh, how she wished a hole would open up and swallow her away. Here she was in her fine blue velvet dress, just married to the man of her dreams, and she up and fainted.

"Yes." They were only a few yards from the church. Looking over his shoulder, she saw Reverend Crittlestick watching them from the porch. The other two men and the wagon were gone. "How long have I been out?"

"Only a minute or two," he said, setting her on her feet. "Just enough time to say good-bye to Lucky and Francis." He pointed to the rattling wagon. "There they go around the corner."

She didn't want to look. Now the story would be around the town in no time. All of Chance's friends would think she was a silly, brainless ninny. She felt like crying, but that would only make this whole mess worse.

"Can you walk?"

She straightened. Squared her shoulders. "Of course, thank you." She took his arm, and they returned down the street they'd come up less than an hour before. But now they were man and wife. Her mind was blank. So much for good conversation. Why couldn't she think of a single thing to say?

A gun discharged down the block stopping her in her tracks.

"That's just the men in the saloon. They're rowdier since Sheriff Crawford is out of town."

She nodded, still feeling shaky.

He eyed her. "You're not going to faint again, are you? I promise you're safe with me."

"I don't swoon at any old thing, Chance."

"Just spiders?"

"Just spiders." She held her chin up. Remembering her letter to Trudy in her bag, she asked, "Where can I send a post?"

"Just ahead at Lichtenstein's. We'll go inside and I'll show you around."

When they arrived at the store, Chance politely opened the closed bottom half of the Dutch door for Evie. The store was larger than it looked with clusters of merchandise everywhere.

"Over there by the cash register is where you'll post your letter. It should go out on today's stage." He pointed to the far wall. "Canned goods there, on the right, hardware. Lichtenstein has some dress material in the back, but you'll find more across the street at Berta May's sewing shop. Everything else on the shelves is placed in alphabetical order."

He took her shoulders and turned her around to the shelf. "Almonds next to alum powder for pickling, and so on. Over there, candy is next to the hair combs. Mr. Lichtenstein is very organized. If you need something, just start at this end at the As and continue around the room. You'll come to it sooner or later."

"That's fine if you know the alphabet." Agitation from fainting, and her too tight corset, still had her insides tangled, but Chance hadn't seemed to notice.

"Guess you're right." He lightened his tone. "But one thing I do know about you is you're an educated woman, and I have the letters to prove it."

A man, ancient as the pyramids in Egypt and clad in overalls with big black boots, shuffled in their direction. "That's ol' Mr. Simpson," Chance whispered. "Store clerk." He looked around. "Don't see Mr. Lichtenstein here."

"Can I help ya find somethin', missy?" As the clerk came closer, he gave a wave of his wrinkly hand. "Oh, didn't see ya, Chance. Blended right in with the store-bought shirts hanging on the wall."

"Mr. Simpson, my wife has a letter she'd like to send."

The old man's face brightened.

Taking the hanky from her sleeve, Evie folded the cloth into a small rectangle. She slipped it into her open letter and sealed the envelope, patting the flap for several seconds.

Mr. Simpson scuffled behind the long counter totally missing the fact that Chance had called Evie his wife. He took the letter, looked at the address a long time, then marked the three-cent stamp with the carved end of a cork he'd carefully dipped in ink. The cancellation was a distinct YK.

"Do you know when my post will reach St. Louis?"

The clerk rubbed his chin. "That's hard to tell."

Evie hardly heard his response. A poster tacked to the wall behind Mr. Simpson's head made her eyes go wide and her heart painfully thwack against her rib cage.

ATTENTION!

STEALING MAIL IS A FEDERAL CRIME.

OFFENDERS WILL BE PROSECUTED.

She gulped.

She hadn't known.

The letters! Mrs. Seymour! But...but Chance's first letter had to go to someone, didn't it? Will the finding fee I left behind be enough to satisfy the mistress so she doesn't turn me in? I left plenty to pay for two weeks' board. Isn't that the same as if Mrs. Seymour made the match herself?

A sense of relief calmed her when she remembered no one besides Trudy knew where she was, or where to find her. Who could bring charges?

"Evie," Chance said, looking earnestly into her face. "I didn't want to ask, but now that we're married, I think I will. Did you receive my last post? The silly one with the small yellow buttercup?"

Turning, she gaped. "Buttercup?"

He chuckled. "It didn't say much of anything. Just that I was counting the days until you arrived."

"No." She could only whisper, her throat tight.

Mr. Simpson came around the counter to stand close.

"You have any smelling salts?" Chance asked.

She hardly noticed his rueful smile. All her warm feelings evaporated and the objects in the store, which moments before had enticed and delighted, now swam before her eyes. *Chance sent another letter? Mrs. Seymour will know where I am. Am I a criminal? Will she come after me?*

Chance winked when the old man scurried off to find smelling salts. "It never hurts to be prepared. Might be a spider or two out at the ranch."

She gave him a weak smile, barely hearing his words.

Chance's hand on her lower back brought her to reality. "I'm gettin' hungry," he said. "How about you?"

"No. Uh, I mean yes." She could see he was trying to figure her out. "A little, I guess."

"You want to go to the Biscuit Barrel for a piece of pie?"

All Evie wanted to do was get out of town where she didn't feel conspicuous and vulnerable. Was some marshal on her trail already? That poster had rocked her to her soul. She didn't like looking over her shoulder all the time, wondering what might happen next. It was like waiting for the ax to fall—on her neck. "When are we going out to the ranch, Chance? I'm so looking forward to seeing it." Her voice was tight. "Settle in."

He gave her a strange look. "Well, actually, I'll be going out there after we eat. I have the dog to tend, heifers to check, and a few other things to do. That might take a day or two."

"A day or two?" She tried not to show her disappointment, or shock.

He nodded. "I want to—ah—give you an opportunity to get to know me better before taking you out where the birds and cattle are your only neighbors for miles."

"That's kind, but not necessary. I *want* to be alone with you." That slipped out before she realized how inappropriate it sounded. Her face heated.

His face turned bright red right before her eyes.

"I-I can *help* you with whatever needs doing. Many hands make light work. Whatever needs doing will be finished in half the time."

Chance straightened and looked around, avoiding her gaze.

He must think her forward and uncouth. Or, too, he was remembering her reaction to the creepy daddy longlegs and was having second thoughts about his prissy wife. How could she make him understand she wasn't a shrinking violet about anything—except spiders? She *liked* to work.

"Nope. Not today, Evie, and most likely not tomorrow either. I ran into a small hitch in my schedule, but plan to remedy that soon."

"Schedule?"

He tipped her chin up with a finger. "You'll be much more comfortable here at the hotel where you can rest properly, meet some of the ladies in town, socialize a little."

"But, Chance…"

His expression said she'd not sweet-talk him into anything. Or change his mind. "I—I don't want to socialize. I want to help you."

With an outstretched arm, he opened the door and let her precede him through. "Mr. Simpson, I'll be back later for the smelling salts," he called over her head. "That's nice of you, Evie, but I'm putting my foot down on this. A few days in town will be a treat."

Chapter Twelve

Holy smokes saints alive! When Evie took aim with her pleading baby blues, his insides crumbled and his breath came fast. He'd have to be made of stronger stuff than this to resist her for long. Hold fast to his ideals and not sway to her doing.

It was best. The house would be finished, come heck or high water, before he carried her over the threshold—*just like I promised.* He was a man of his word. The roof would be on and the bedroom door in place before she hung her HOME SWEET HOME plate above the soon-to-be river rock mantel.

"This way," he said, leading her across the dusty road. He paused to avoid a wagon, then hurried her along as two horses passed behind. They made their way toward the Biscuit Barrel amid looks from the good citizens. "We'll stop in here and eat." Her lips were just so darn kissable. Ever since this morning at their wedding, kissing her again was practically all he could think about. He took a quick glance down to find her gazing up at him.

"Chance? *Please.*"

"It's for the *best,* Evie. Nothing you can say will change my mind." *Is this our first disagreement?*

They were past the Hitching Post Saloon when the clank of a door closing sounded behind them. "Well, I'll be a blue bunny," a sexy voice said teasingly. "If it's not Mr. and Mrs. Holcomb in the flesh."

"Fancy!" Evie exclaimed.

That sultry purr belonged to one woman alone. Chance turned.

"I'm delighted to see you," Evie said, hurrying to her side. "Chance and I got married this morning in the church."

"Congratulations," Fancy Aubrey said, flicking her saucy gaze to him. "That little gold band did catch my eye."

Fancy's light green dress molded to her body like a calf's hide after a rainstorm. Her plunging neckline was so low, he had to look everywhere but at her breasts spilling out over the top.

Evie held her hand out, admiring the ring, apparently oblivious to the look of envy on the older woman's face. Evie lowered her hand, then looked through the window of the saloon as if just now realizing where her friend had come from. Her confused expression brought a soft chuckle from Fancy.

"Yes, it's true, sugar. I'm a *saloon* girl. For shame, for shame."

"Oh, I didn't realize when we—"

"I'm sure you didn't. Most women won't walk on the same side of the street as me if they know who I am, let alone have a nice, down-home conversation. They don't like me. Always afraid I'm gonna try to steal their men." She batted her eyelashes at Chance.

He didn't like the direction this conversation was headed. *This woman is trouble in one form or another.* "Have you settled in, Miss Aubrey?" he asked, trying to change the subject. Several men could be seen through the saloon window, lined up against the bar as Abe poured another round. It was only ten in the morning.

She smiled. "Call me Fancy."

She wasn't making this easy.

"Not walk down the street with you? Why, that's ridiculous!" Evie exclaimed. She straightened and tipped her head angrily. "You wouldn't steal someone's husband. Everyone has to have a job, and it shouldn't define who you are. A saloon is as good a place to work as any. Some people can be so small-minded."

Was Evie so naive as to think whiskey pouring and card shuffling were all Fancy Aubrey did to earn her pay?

"Why, Chance and I would be delighted if you came out to our house for—"

"Evie," Chance said quickly, cutting her off. "If I don't get something into my belly soon, I won't be fit company." He gave Fancy a don't-fool-with-my-wife look and took Evie's arm. Evie would be cut off completely from Y Knot society if she opened her home to the town's new lady of the night. Sad, but true. If he could change the world, he would. But as things stood, good, respectable women didn't associate with saloon girls. Period. Nor did they befriend other women who did associate with them.

"But, Chance."

"You go on, sugar, before Mr. Holcomb faints away," Miss Aubrey said before he could respond. She backed toward the swinging doors. "I wouldn't want to be the cause of making you a widow so soon after your wedding."

"But…"

Hurt welled up in Evie's eyes. Chance knew his wife didn't understand what he was doing, just that he was treating her new friend like the other closed-minded citizens Evie had just been bemoaning. *Well, better hurt and confused now, than ostracized later.* He'd explain in detail when they had more time, and knew each other a little better.

After a satisfying meal followed by pie at the Biscuit Barrel, Chance walked Evie back to her hotel room and unlocked the door. Not even the apple cobbler she'd eaten could quiet the butterflies now fluttering inside her. This was their first time alone, in a room, since becoming man and wife. Would Chance kiss her? A real kiss? One that stopped the rain or changed the course of a river? He looked a little nervous as he walked over to the window, opened it, and looked out.

He turned to face her. "The day is still young and I need to ride out to the ranch and check on the cattle. Have one calf born, with nine to go. I need to see how they're doing."

She hurried to his side. "Can't I go too, Chance? I'm anxious to see the place, put my things away." She glanced to her carpetbag, a little embarrassed she didn't have more to offer. "I won't get in the way. I promise."

He shifted his weight, and his brows drew down over his eyes. "Not today, Evie. Remember what I said about me putting the place to right. I'm just not quite ready for you yet. Soon, though."

When she opened her mouth, he shushed her with a soft touch of a finger to her lips. "My mind's made up. You won't change it."

Disappointment crushed her. The morning had been beautiful, then the time spent with Chance at the restaurant after the wedding was one of the best times she could remember. He'd had her laughing at the silliest things. Who knew a cowboy could be so funny?

Fidgeting with the sash of her dress, she said, "Fine. I guess I understand." Why hadn't he tried to kiss her, hold her? Did he find her attractive at all? It was so hard to know what to do.

"Evie," he said, his tone contrite.

She willed away tears. "Have I done something wrong?"

"No. Nothing like that. I told you why. A few things out at the—" A shadow crossed his face. "Aww, don't cry."

When he enfolded her in his embrace, she melted against his chest. Her heart galloped as his scent drew her deeper. She wrapped her arms around his waist and they stood motionless, the sounds of the street drifting in through the window.

He pulled back. Gazed into her eyes. Lowered his face to hers.

When his lips finally touched hers, her eyes drifted closed, but not for long. The kiss was soft, short, and all too soon moved to her forehead where he placed a brief caress before pulling away.

"I'll try to be back tomorrow afternoon, but don't panic if I'm not. Just means I'm involved with the cattle. I've arranged for the room until, well, until—" He paused.

She nodded, wiping her eyes with the back of her hand. "I'm sorry I got emotional. I don't want to make things harder for you. I'm supposed to be a help, not a hindrance. Just know that, I'll be here until you come for me. You needn't worry about getting back quickly. Just take care of what you need to do."

A gunshot blast rattled the wall from across the street in the saloon and she leapt instinctively back into his arms. Raucous laughter sounded through the open window.

With a twinge of embarrassment, she pulled away. "I know. Just the men letting off steam since the sheriff is gone." She looked up into his eyes. "I'll get used to it soon enough."

But she wondered if her words were true. She'd been brought up in St. Louis, with the Victorian house—the agency—being the center of her world. She rarely left the premises, except to go to the farmers market twice a week, and then for a walk to the library now and then on her day off. Before her death, her mother had schooled Evie. She knew little of a wild Western town, except what she'd read from dime novels. She chanced a look out. "Do they ever do more than let off steam?"

"Not usually. But I'll have a talk with Deputy Jones before I leave town. If you venture out, best you stay on this side of the street."

Chapter Thirteen

Fiddlesticks! Wearing her brown dress, Evie walked past the mercantile *again*, the poster above the postal desk drawing her gaze like a magnet. If she closed her eyes, she could probably recall every last item displayed in the store's window. She'd been up and down this street so many times she'd lost count. She was bored. True to his word, and to her disappointment, Chance had not shown up this morning. Whatever he had to do out at the ranch must be important.

Maybe she should go back to the hotel and have a cup of tea. That would pass a good half hour. *Tea.* That exciting thought made her think of Mrs. Klinkner, and her invitation. What if she walked over to her house for a visit right now? The woman had been insistent with her offer. Evie looked left, then right. Where was Creek Street? Couldn't be that hard to find. She tapped her chin.

After asking directions, Evie found herself on Creek Street. The rural road wound down a slight incline and through some trees toward an open area. Instead of horses neighing and the rumble of wagon wheels, or even gun blasts, she heard the happy chirping of birds in the trees, the trickling of water, the swoosh of the wind as it rocked the high boughs of a nearby grove of pine trees. There were a few houses set back off the road, but by and large, the street was more country lane than town, and a delightful change.

A team of black horses pulling a lone wagon came in her direction. The horses slowed from a trot to a walk, then stopped a few feet from where she stood. Evie was now painfully aware of how secluded she felt.

"'Scuse me," the middle-aged man said. He wore a bright red flannel shirt with the sleeves rolled up his forearms. "You need a ride or somethin'?"

She pointed to herself and then looked around. "Me, sir?"

"You the only one here that I see."

Uncertain, she took a tiny step away. "No, thank you. I'm headed to the lumber mill."

"In that case, just keep on going straight. You're almost there. I don't usually see anyone out this way 'cept Mrs. Klinkner, is why I asked."

She kicked out her skittering nerves and smiled. "Thank you. That was kind."

He doffed his hat. "Good day." He slapped the reins and his horses started off.

She'd been so deep in thought, dreaming about Chance and enjoying nature everywhere she looked, that she hadn't noticed how remote this street really was. She'd do well to keep her wits about her in the future. This was Montana, not the busy streets of St. Louis. The lack of traffic and hustle and bustle had relaxed her. She'd let down her guard. She needed to start thinking like a Westerner. Maybe there were wolves or bears just beyond, lurking in the trees. She hastened her step.

The buzzing sound of a saw chased away her apprehension. She picked up her pace when the mill and a quaint two-story house across the road from it, came into view.

Relieved, she patted her drooping hair and straightened her skirt. Taking a breath for courage, she strode up the walkway and knocked on the door. A few moments passed before it opened and a mouthwatering aroma spilled out.

"Why, Evie, hello," Mrs. Klinkner said in surprise. "It's wonderful to see you, dear." She looked out the door, then over to the lumber mill. "Did you get married? Is Chance with you?"

Evie laughed. "Yes and no. We got married yesterday morning." She held out her ring proudly. "But Chance had some things to do at the ranch, so while he's working, I thought I'd pay a social call. I hope you don't mind my coming unannounced."

Mrs. Klinkner swooped Evie into a tight hug. "Of course not, child. Things in Montana are a lot less formal than St. Louis, I'd guess. Nobody sends calling cards here—we just drop in when we find time between chores." She stepped away, motioning for Evie to enter. "And I'm delighted you did. In the hotel, I practically begged you to come out. I'm so happy you took the invitation to heart. Now, let's go into the kitchen and I'll put the kettle on. I was just about to take a cake out of the oven."

Evie followed behind, taking in the loveliness of the house. The parlor was beautiful. Finely carved shelves and hutches were everywhere, each filled with colorful knickknacks. *Dusting and polishing must take hours!* Long, lovely drapes, done in cheerful blue and lavender, adorned the tall parlor windows. *Oh, to have a home like this.*

"Here we are," the woman said as they entered a cozy room toward the back of the house. It was half the size of the kitchen she was used to, but had all the amenities a woman could need. Pleasant yellow walls were decorated with plants and keepsakes, and a bank of windows filled the room with light. Evie stopped to admire everything before her eyes.

"Just pull up a chair and I'll get this started. What have you been doing since we last talked?"

"Mostly just strolling up and down the street," Evie said, settling herself in a chair by the window. "When I thought about having a cup of tea in the restaurant, I thought of you, Mrs. Klinkner."

"I'm happy you did—but first, you must call me Ina, I insist. Did you walk?"

"Yes. Wasn't that far."

"I do it all the time. It's good for my health and gives me time to think. Sometimes it's the only solitude I have, with the customers coming and going at the lumber mill all day long."

Evie nodded. The woman moved about with efficiency. Taking potholders, she slid two brimming round pans out of the oven, and placed them on a cooling rack on the counter by the window. "There."

"Beautiful," Evie said, getting up and coming close. "Smells delicious. I noticed the aroma first thing when I walked through the door." A new idea took hold. Would Mrs. Klinkner teach her how to bake a cake? If so, could she be proficient in three weeks' time?

A soft grinding noise sounded above the sink, and then a small wooden bird popped out of a cuckoo clock's tiny red door, followed by a pretty cooing sound. Mrs. Klinkner looked up, surprised. "Oh, the men will be here momentarily."

"Are they working on Saturday?"

"Oh, yes. When you own a business, you have to make hay while the sun shines, as they say."

"I'll go then," Evie said, sad to leave this cheerful place.

"Oh, no. We haven't had our tea yet. Just let me set out their meal and then we'll have our visit."

Torn, Evie didn't know what to say. The book on etiquette said when making a call it wasn't proper to stay more than twenty minutes or less than ten. Thirteen minutes had already passed since her arrival, and if she stayed until the men came, then had tea, surely it would be more like an hour. The last thing she wanted to be was a bother to her new friend. "Only if you're sure."

"Absolutely. Now, you just get comfortable and I'll have this out in no time."

The woman was a whirlwind of movement. Right before Evie's eyes, the table took shape; platters of cooked meat, sliced bread, and cut vegetables were set out. She poured two cups of coffee and set them by the plates. Finished, she took a deep breath. "There. I eat after the men are gone, taking time to enjoy myself. They are usually in and out in fifteen minutes."

"Mr. Klinkner and your son Hayden?"

The woman's smile brightened. "Why, yes. That's right. You have a good memory."

Evie heard the sound of voices and the front door opened.

Mr. Klinkner came in, followed by a young man broad of shoulder and with a thick head of yellow hair. Stubble covered his jaw almost as completely as sawdust covered his shoulders. Mr. Klinkner wore denim overalls, but Hayden wore pants so tight she thought they must be uncomfortable.

Heat from within blazed Evie's face. Both men pulled up short when they saw her.

"Hello," Hayden said. A small dimple dotted his left cheek as his lips pulled up in an enticing, but devilish, smile.

"This is the gal I told you about yesterday," Mr. Klinkner said, giving her a face-splitting smile. "The delightful young woman from St. Louis we met in the restaurant." He looked smaller in his work garments, different from when she'd seen him in his fancy dinner clothes. A kerchief replaced the bow tie and his face was sweaty from work. "I'm glad you've come to visit us, Miss Davenport."

"It's Mrs. Holcomb now." Mrs. Klinkner hurried over and placed a warm hand on each of Evie's shoulders. "Chance and Evie married up yesterday."

"Well, I'll be," Hayden said slowly. His brows arched over his piercing blue eyes and his lips curled up even more. He bowed showily and Evie didn't know how to respond. "I'm pleased to make your acquaintance. I'd say Chance is one lucky cowboy, much more so than he deserves."

What a strange thing to say. After Chance's reaction to him the day she arrived, she'd bet there was no love lost between them.

"Hayden," Mrs. Klinkner said. "How many times have I asked you to dust off before coming in?" She clucked her tongue. "Sit down gently so as not to set those shavings flying." She pulled out his chair and he took his place at the table without taking his eyes off Evie. Mrs. Klinkner served both men a generous serving of each dish, after which Mr. Klinkner offered a short blessing.

"Evie and I are going to take our tea into the parlor. Just call if there's anything else you need." The woman picked up the tray she'd prepared while waiting for the men, then disappeared through the doorway. Evie quickly followed.

Chapter Fourteen

Chance muscled open the tall barn doors and went inside, Dexter trotting at his heels. The tangy stench of skunk had weakened considerably, but the dog still acted shamefaced every time Chance looked at him. One by one, he pulled tarps off the few large pieces of furniture he owned, mostly handmade by himself, for inspection. There wasn't much. A table and four chairs he'd made last year. A desk, two stools. A used stove he'd purchased three months ago.

The bed, too cumbersome to go through any doorway, had been built inside the large bedroom, facing a window that looked out on the front pasture. It, too, was covered in oilcloth since the gray-blue sky clouded up yesterday with the promise of rain. Satisfied with the way things looked, he ambled outside, oblivious to the pitter-patter on his felt Stetson or the light drops wetting his clothes. From the paddock, his saddle horse looked his way briefly, then lowered his head back to the grass.

Another calf had arrived last night, born in the wee hours without incident. The Charolais were proving to be exactly what they were known for, and he was thankful. He'd hate to lose a single one. Dexter had alerted him, already asleep in a bedroll on the floor of the house. The dog had nudged his master with his cold, wet nose, then whined unceasingly until he'd taken notice. He hadn't had far to go to find the heifer and new baby. He felt like a proud papa.

Perhaps time had come to tell Evie the truth. Just explain what had happened with the nails. In his excitement, he had gotten ahead of himself telling her the house was done, as he'd wholeheartedly expected. It wasn't really a lie. If there was anything he could do to get the place finished now, he'd do it. Yesterday Lichtenstein had no new news for him.

He missed her. A day without his wife seemed like a week. Her face had colored pink, prettier than snow flowers poking out of the ground in November, when she'd told him she wanted to be alone with him. *Imagine that.* He took a deep breath, then lifted his face to the sky to have it kissed by the light rain.

Things might not be all that bad if she came out, camped, helped work on getting the house finished. She may even enjoy the experience.

Don't kid yourself, Holcomb, an annoying voice taunted. A city girl afraid of spiders ain't going to want to camp. She's used to that two-story mansion in St. Louis.

Still, just her being around would make him happier, and he'd want to work that much faster. Hell, truth be known, he didn't know when Lichtenstein would get any nails in. It could be months! Keeping her in town that long would bleed his bank account dry.

Back in town, and feeling much happier after her visit with Ina, Evie headed toward the hotel. If she couldn't be with Chance, she'd be sure to be ready when he did come calling.

The time was only a little past noon. Maybe he would miss her. Come into town for dinner at the restaurant. A girl could dream.

About to enter the hotel, she stopped when a man appeared out of Lichtenstein's Provisions and hurried her way. "Mrs. Holcomb?"

"Yes, that's me." Living in a small town did have some advantages. Seemed many people knew who she was without even being introduced.

He smiled and nodded, then pushed his spectacles up the bridge of his short nose. "I am Herr Lichtenstein. Proprietor of the mercantile next door. It's my pleasure to meet you. I've been waiting for your return."

"Thank you." He must have asked for her in the hotel where she'd let the clerk know she was going to Mrs. Klinkner's, just in case Chance came looking for her. "I'm pleased to meet you, too."

His face beamed. Seemed he couldn't get the words out fast enough. "Please tell Chance that the nails he's been waiting on arrived today by freight wagon." His wrinkled hands fairly shook with eagerness, and he clamped them together, weaving his fingers. "Fifty pounds. Plenty to complete the whole house. I'm sure you are as anxious as he is to get your new home finished so you can move in. I apologize the construction has taken this long. He's been checking with me daily, as well as riding all over the countryside trying to find some."

Nails?

Finish the house?

Poor Chance! He hadn't wanted to tell her after she'd gushed so much about having a new home to move in to, that the house wasn't finished. "Yes, I'll tell him," she answered as soon as she found her voice.

Beyond his shoulder, she saw Francis coming down the street in a wagon and another cowboy riding alongside. They reined up, and the cowboy dismounted and left in the opposite direction. Did she dare do what was whispering in her heart?

"Thank you so much for letting me know, Mr. Lichtenstein. I'll tell Chance the moment I see him," she said quickly. "I'm very sorry to rush off, but I must speak with Mr., er, Francis, before he slips away. I see him down the street." The shopkeeper smiled happily, nodding his agreement as she breezed past.

The moment the boy saw her coming, he turned and started across the street toward the leather smith's. If she didn't hurry, she might miss her only opportunity to help Chance. "Francis," she called. When he didn't respond, she tried a bit louder and crossed the street after him.

When she called a third time, garnering several townspeople's attention, propriety insisted he stop and turn around. "Ma'am?"

She stopped by his side and lowered her skirt. This town was dustier than St. Louis. His scared, ready-to-bolt expression almost made her laugh. "I never got a chance to thank you properly for standing up for Chance and me at the wedding yesterday. You were very good-natured about the whole affair, holding my flowers and all."

He scuffed his boot on the boardwalk and a line of red slowly started up his neck.

"Especially when I saw the spider." Just saying the creepy word sent a shiver up the back of her legs. "I'm sorry if I frightened you with all my screaming."

"No, you didn't scare me, ma'am. It was my pleasure to help."

"Really?"

"Sure."

She felt a bit guilty about having ulterior motives when he was so shy and charming.

"Lucky and me like Chance a lot. He's family."

She nodded encouragingly when he relaxed and uncrossed his arms. She even thought one corner of his lips lifted up in a smile.

"Family?"

Francis pushed his hat up and gave her his first real smile, one that went all the way to his eyes. "Sure, he lived with us for years in the McCutcheon bunkhouse. It don't feel quite the same since he left. Why, he still signs on and helps with the big fall drive once a year."

"I didn't know all that. Thank you. I have so much to learn."

"My pleasure. If you need anything else, just let me know…"

He must have read something in her face. His head tipped away and a wary expression crossed his eyes.

It's now or never. "Actually there *is* something, Francis. I would like to ask for one more helping hand, if that's all right with you. I don't know who else to turn to."

His Adam's apple bobbed. "What is it?"

"Chance is out at the ranch checking on the cattle since they are having babies."

"Calving."

"Yes, that's right. Well, Mr. Lichtenstein just told me the nails Chance is waiting for just came in. Do you think you might give me a ride out there, so we can deliver them? I'd like to surprise him. It would mean so much."

Francis glanced over at his wagon, and the horse tied at the hitching rail beside it. "Don't know. Roady and me came into town to pick up a couple of saddles getting repaired and need to get back to the ranch."

She nibbled her bottom lip. "I see." She glanced around. "Well, thank you all the same. I'm sure it's a long way out of your way. I know you would if you could."

When she turned to leave, he stopped her. "Mrs. Holcomb?"

"Evie."

His face flamed. "Where're the nails?"

She couldn't stop a smile from bursting onto her face. "At the mercantile."

"I'll pick 'em up right as soon as I get the saddles and then let Roady know where I'm going."

"Thank you! I'll just run over to the hotel and get my few things and be ready to go in five minutes. I'll wait for you at your wagon. Thank you so much, Francis. I can't tell you how much this means to me. Chance is going to be so surprised to see us both."

Chapter Fifteen

Finished with all he could do for now, Chance saddled his horse and mounted up, ignoring the dark clouds threatening above. The spattering rain had stopped yesterday, but a cool wind pushed at his clothes and chilled his skin.

Dexter barked with excitement.

"Nope, you're not going," he said, anxious to get back to town and Evie. The dog trotted back and forth excitedly, ready to go out to check the cattle. He wasn't going to like being left behind again. "I'll be back out tomorrow." He pointed to the house. "Stay."

Dexter's head dropped and his ears flattened against his fur when he realized he wasn't going anywhere. Chance almost smiled.

He was sore. Residual aches and pains from sleeping on the floor nagged him. On top of that, thoughts of Evie had kept him awake most of the night, so he was tired and grumpy. He needed to get back to her. Talk with her. Hold her hand in his.

With a soft cluck, and pressure from his leg, he maneuvered his horse in a half circle and eased him into a lope down the winding wagon track toward Y Knot. Wide rolling hills dotted with oak and pine, plus iron-tough chaparral, so worrisome to a newborn calf's tender hide, stretched out as far as the eye could see.

The view never grew old. It was good land. *Their land.* Every time he traveled it, pride of ownership warmed his soul. Maybe today would be the day the nails arrived. If that happened, he'd hire all the extra hands he could find, regardless of the cost, and get the house completed. Evie was being darn agreeable. How many other newly wedded women would stay alone in an unfamiliar town?

Rounding the bend, he sat back in his saddle, his mount sliding to a halt. Surprise made him blink several times, grit from no sleep making him wince. He didn't know if he was seeing things, or his deep desire to see Evie had conjured her up out of thin air.

A wagon approached. The conveyance rocked back and forth with the gentle hills and dips of the terrain. Francis drove with Evie next to him, and Roady Guthrie, the McCutcheon's silver-tongued foreman, rode his horse alongside. Chance's first delight at seeing his wife dissipated with a snap of anger. He cautioned himself to rein in his temper. Just because he asked her to wait for him in town and said no to her many eye-batting, soft-voiced requests to come, didn't mean she had to mind him. But it did mean he wanted her to, that she *should.* Couldn't she take no for an answer?

She's not a slave, Holcomb, he reminded himself. Still. Here she was now, right before his eyes, as if she didn't have a care in the world. In a few minutes, she'd see the unfinished state of affairs she believed was her new home, and there was nothing he could do to stop her.

When they were within hearing distance, he called out. "Francis, Roady. You're a far cry from the Heart of the

Mountains. What brings you out this way, boys?" He gestured to the stormy sky, and the broiling black clouds above.

Evie's keen gaze studied him. The finely shaped lips he'd been dreaming about all night long, the ones he longed to kiss right now, pulled down at the corners. Perhaps she could feel his anger all the way over to the wagon seat.

"Found ourselves a traveler," Roady said with a laugh. "She asked for a ride out to the ranch. We were only too happy to oblige."

"I can see." He couldn't stop the way her gaze drew him like a magnet, the way a handful of oats drew his horse. Was he a sap, to be pulled this way and that?

Francis brought the team to a halt when the wagon reached him. A light wrap was all Evie had to keep off the cold bite of the wind. Her apple-red nose looked painful. Anger zipped through his insides again, making him clamp his teeth together and look away.

"Chance?" Evie said.

Several seconds passed, the wind nipping the top of his ears. Was she tongue-tied? Well, good. She should be. He was the man of the house. She needed to listen to what he said. Respect his wishes. No mistaking, Roady and Francis thought the turn of events quite amusing.

"Trouble in paradise?" Roady's all-knowing smile stretched Chance's already taut nerves to a breaking point.

Francis closed his mouth.

"I—" She hesitated. "I have a message from Mr. Lichtenstein at the store."

He shifted in the saddle. He'd checked with the shop owner yesterday. "Go on."

"The nails you ordered came in. He was very pleased because he knows how important they are to you and how you've been trying to get the house done before I arrived." She stopped and took a long breath. "Anyway, they're here. In the back."

The nails had finally arrived?

Chance shot a look into the wagon bed. It hadn't even crossed his mind that there might be another reason for her appearance. Shock registered when he recognized her carpetbag next to a large wooden crate. *She's planning to stay? Now? To camp outside? With me?* An uncomfortable warmth moved through his chest, then up into his face. "Fifty pounds?" he asked. Meanwhile, his mind was racing.

"You bet," Roady answered. "Fifty pounds down to the last nail. Along with some hardware you've been waiting on. Now, get out of the way so we can get up to the homestead and unload."

Before moving his horse, he slipped off his jacket and handed the heavy garment to Evie. "Put this on before you freeze."

She took the coat without complaint and slipped it on, the weighty leather engulfing her. He turned his horse. She'd come with the nails. Still, he could have picked them up himself and gotten the house finished this week, as he'd planned. Darn, if he didn't hate to have her see the half-finished home now.

They continued on and soon Dexter raced out to meet them.

"There she is, Mrs. Holcomb," Roady said, pointing. He had her complete attention. "That's the house. The smokehouse and well. Over there's the barn, windmill, and some livestock paddocks." He looked over to Chance. "You've done a fine job, Holcomb. Looks well-thought-out. I like it."

Chance stepped his horse forward. "I'm glad you like it, Roady."

Francis shot Roady a look.

Chance had wanted to be the one to show her everything; now it was Roady who was doing the showing, pointing things out.

"As a matter of fact," Chance added a bit sardonically. "I did want to get *your* opinion on the house placement, and the size of the barn."

Grasping his meaning instantly, Roady scowled. "You hold on a minute," he barked. "We didn't come out here to start any trouble. We were just being neighborly when your wife asked for a ride. Hell, I can take her back if you want."

Chapter Sixteen

Evie's heart lurched with regret as she took in Chance's dark, angry eyes and slate-hard expression. He wore a gun strapped to his thigh, and a rifle, encased in leather, hung from his saddle. She stilled the urge to scamper for cover. Sorrow over killing the sweet feelings building between them bruised her heart. Still, her delight over her first glimpse of the ranch made her clamp her hand over her mouth and her eyes go wide. Her wildest dreams couldn't touch the beauty of the house—even unfinished. And the setting stole her breath. The sky stretched so far and looked so mystical. Oh, how she'd been blessed! Such a man, a home, a life. Had she ruined everything by disobeying him? Maybe he'd send her packing even without finding out about her past. Her stomach churned, threatening to spill out Ina's delicious cookies.

"Don't get mouthy with me," Chance shot back at Roady.

She should have listened to him. Stayed put until he was ready for her. "I was only trying to help." Her comment, offered softly from the wagon seat, fell on deaf ears. She'd thought that after his surprise at seeing her, he'd be pleased she was trying to be useful. Delivering the nails had saved him hours, maybe even half a day. Instead, he looked cross.

Roady stiffened. "You're a stubborn fool. If your wife weren't here, Holcomb, I'd teach you a lesson in manners."

"I didn't mean to cause an argument," Evie added, hoping for forgiveness. She'd learned on the ride out from Y Knot that Roady also worked for the McCutcheon ranch and lived in the bunkhouse too. They all were close friends—or used to be.

"Here, Mrs. Holcomb, let me help you down. Your husband can't seem to remember his manners." Roady held out his hand and waited for her to take it. She didn't want to. Didn't want to add fuel to the fire, so to speak.

"Go on, Dexter, get back," Roady said to the dog whose shrill barks and yips filled the air.

Having no other choice, she took the proffered help and climbed out of the wagon, feeling awkward and conspicuous. With her dress and Chance's coat, the task proved more difficult than it should. When her feet were safely on the ground, she sent up a silent prayer of thanks that she hadn't made a complete fool of herself by falling on her head. She hefted Chance's large coat up around her shoulders, his musky scent and the blessed warmth the only good things, besides her lovely visit with Ina, about this day so far.

At her feet, the friendly dog Roady had called Dexter dropped to his haunches and gazed up at her with adoration. His dancing eyes invited her touch, but suddenly the unmistakable skunk scent made her quickly step back and pull her hand away. She gasped, and clamped her hand over her mouth and nose.

Chance dismounted and tied his horse to the hitching rail. Heading for the barn, he gave a short whistle and Dexter bolted to his side.

"Oh, he got sprayed good this time," Francis said with a laugh. "That dog gives that skunk more trouble."

Chance pointed and the dog obediently slunk into the barn. Chance pushed closed the tall wooden doors, then headed back.

"Probably chasing him at night. Dogs can hardly resist their scent," Francis said, then followed Roady to the back of the wagon. As Francis reached for her bag, Roady grasped the wooden crate of nails and set it on the porch.

"Let's go, Francis. Chance is in a foul mood." Roady looked at her. "You sure you wouldn't rather go back into Y Knot? We don't mind taking you."

She shook her head. "No, thank you. I do appreciate you bringing me out."

A bark sounded from the barn. They all turned as Chance walked up.

"We'll get out of your hair now."

Chance nodded, the anger in his expression was gone. "I appreciate you delivering the nails," he said. "My wife, too."

Her heart fluttered. Did he mean it? Or was he just being polite in front of the cowboys? She remembered his kiss, his hands on her waist, his expression as he'd said his vows. She'd make this up to him, if he'd just give her the chance.

Francis climbed onto the wagon seat and Roady mounted his horse. "You have your work cut out for you," Roady said, gesturing to the half-built structure and the stack of tarp-covered lumber. "Yep, you sure do." He turned his horse as Francis set the wagon rolling.

"Good-bye," Evie called, waving her hand. She felt tiny next to Chance in the wide openness of the valley. Being used to the city, with streets full of people talking and the clamor of folks coming and going, she found this desolate—and a bit frightening. "Thank you, again."

Roady's good-hearted chuckle floated back to them. "Next time I see you, Mrs. Holcomb, I'll ask you if you're still thankful." His laughter filled the air.

The nervous energy radiating off Chance was palpable. She turned and faced him, ready for the dressing down she was sure to come.

"So," she said softly, wanting to break the ice. A burst of cold blew past her with enough force to ruffle the hair under the brim of his hat. His cheeks were rosier than she'd ever seen them. He had to be cold. "Here, take this." She began to unfasten the buttons when he reached over and placed his large hand on hers.

Heat sizzled where his fingers touched, and lingered. Her breath caught as she looked up into his face. Did he feel it? Was he attracted to her at all? Had she ruined everything between them?

"No. I have another coat in the barn. You keep this on."

"Chance, I'm sorry."

He nodded, then looked away, his hands still warm on hers. They were large and callused, chapped by the wind. Standing so close, she was tempted to wrap her arms around his middle and bury her face into his chest, but didn't dare.

"I'm the one who's sorry," he finally said. "I told you the house was done, because I thought it would be. The bargain was I'd have a place for you, a home. I've let you down."

He was mad at himself? Not at her? "But I came out even though you told me to stay in Y Knot."

"I am a bit annoyed with you for that. Montana isn't St. Louis. It's dangerous country out here. How is this going to work if you don't do what I tell you?"

Evie couldn't stop a smile. She leaned in closer. Pulled one hand away from his and cupped his cheek. "Chance, I wanted to help, that's all. I don't want to be treated like some hothouse flower that needs coddling. I'm telling you now, so please listen and believe. I know how to work—I *like* to work." *Should I tell him the truth? Right now? What would he think if I did?* "I want to be part of the team that gets this place built." She glanced over at the boards and studs that would someday be their home. "It's already beautiful, Chance. I can only imagine how lovely the structure will be when it's complete." She let her hand fall away.

He looked down at the narrow space between them. "That might take a while." His voice was soft and she had to strain to hear him.

"If that happens, so what?" she whispered, inching closer. "We'll build it together."

"Actually, I'm planning on hiring some workers. We'll go into town tomorrow and I'll see whom I can find. That way, it should be finished in a day or two."

She couldn't reply. A yearning so strong took hold and she went up on tiptoe, pressing her mouth to his. Gently, questioningly. For a split second, he didn't respond, and she feared she'd gone and made a fool of herself again. But then he wrapped her in his arms and kissed her passionately, his hands pulling her close, and closer still.

He took a deep breath and stepped back, a lopsided grin appearing on his face. "I hope you like eating jerky and sleeping on the ground."

His eyes were doing funny things to her insides. "The ground?" *With spiders to crawl all over me as I sleep? Nest in my hair?*

"Where else did you think? I camp. Sleep in a bedroll." He glanced to the carpetbag sitting on the porch. "I can't imagine you have a bedroll tucked away in that thing."

She gaped, looking back and forth, before realizing he was teasing her.

He laughed, then took her by the hand. "Don't worry about that now; we'll work it out when night falls. Just so you know, I have a few extra blankets in the barn." He winked and Evie's breath escaped in a small puff. Oh, how she loved Chance, this Chance. Would he always be like this, so understanding, so warm?

"Come on. I want to give you the grand tour."

Chapter Seventeen

Dressed in his extra slicker, Chance straightened and stood, taking one last look at his tools in the barn. He was ready, and itching to get going. He'd finish the house in record time. After showing everything to Evie, pleased by her oohs and aahs over each little detail she saw, he took her out to the barn where she met his three horses, explored the tall loft, and cozied up to Dexter who was sulking in a stall. She begged Chance to let the dog out, saying the smell went away after her nose got used to it. True or not, the animal had taken to her. He devotedly trotted by her heels as if he knew Evie was his deliverer.

Longing for a glimpse of her, Chance went to the barn door and looked out. It took a minute in the waning light, but he finally spotted his wife and Dexter. They were a short distance into the pasture, where she crouched low, proffering an outstretched handful of greenery to two calves standing knee-deep in grass. Their mamas, who'd wandered up toward the barn in the late afternoon ahead of the rest of the herd, grazed nearby.

His heart filled. Marrying Evie was the best thing he'd ever done. Even this soon, he felt it was true. When one of the calves looked her way, she inched forward and the tiny heifer nibbled the grass in her hand. She laughed and the animal bolted away. Glancing over her shoulder, she caught him watching. She smiled and waved.

Twilight eased over the land, calming the breeze and muting the vividness of color. The dark clouds had given way to a gray-blue sky. All they had for supper tonight was a bag of jerky and a half loaf of day-old bread. He hoped the skimpy amount of food would be enough to satisfy her until they went into town first thing tomorrow. From there, he'd go over to Lichtenstein's to see if anyone had been in looking for work. Evie could take some time at the hotel to clean up if she wanted. The day promised to be full.

Dexter barked and Chance quickly looked back to Evie. The rest of the herd was on the move up the valley toward the ranch, coming in for nightfall. Dexter barked again and then bounded out to meet them. As trained, he circled around to the back of the herd, then drove them forward.

When Evie started his way, he went out to join her. The calm evening light was too nice to waste. "How do you like the calves?"

"I don't think I've ever seen anything so cute." Her eyes sparkled and he stifled the urge to reach out and touch her nose. "They look so soft. I'd love to pet them."

"Just keep at it. They'll let you when they get used to you."

"Really?"

"Sure. Cattle can be very domestic. Remember though, they're beef animals and not pets. If they aren't used for breeding, someone's going to eat them."

Her eyes opened wide. He nodded. She needed to know how things worked around here.

They walked along a little farther. "You getting hungry?"

"I am." Her voice was small. She was still thinking about the calves. "But I don't see any restaurants nearby," she said teasingly.

As if the action were commonplace, he took her hand in his and started back toward the house. "You're right about that. The only eatery you'll find around here is—" He paused, thinking. "Hungry Holcomb's Offerings. You'll find the establishment up ahead. One thing though, it's not too good. Only thing on the menu is over-salted jerky and half a loaf of stale bread. But don't despair; I hear tell he's getting a new cook."

Her face blanched, and he wondered what he'd said wrong. Maybe the fact that he wasn't much of a cook and she thought she'd have to do all the work herself. He didn't mind helping, and doing what he knew how. They wouldn't starve by any means, but he did look forward to what she'd have to offer.

He gave her hand a gentle squeeze. Was she nervous being out here alone with him? They walked up the wagon tracks toward the house in silence, him enjoying the feel of her at his side.

A rustling sound at their feet made Evie gasp and grab his hand, jumping behind him as if a dragon had just popped up out of the grass.

He laughed, enjoying her physical touch very much. He could get used to it—and quickly. "That's just a whippoorwill." He pointed to a small brown speckled bird running through the grass. "They nest on the ground and when evening falls, they're everywhere. You'll get used to 'em soon enough."

She'd stopped and watched the bird that was almost invisible. A hand to her heart told him she was rattled. "I guess."

The cattle had settled and Dexter trotted back, wagging his tail. Chance gave her hand a tug. "Come on. I'm hungry myself. I want to eat and get the bedrolls laid out before all the light is gone."

Perched on a chair Chance had brought from the barn, and still snuggled in his large, warm coat, Evie ate a chunk of bread feeling like the Icelandic Viking's woman she'd read about at the library. She had already consumed a slice of jerky—finding the smoky flavor to her liking—then guzzled several long draws of water from his canteen. So far, this new experience of camping with Chance had been exhilarating. She'd helped him lay out the bedding by the light of two lanterns that hung from a beam overhead. Earlier, he'd made several trips to the lumber pile for planks to lay across the massive bed frame constructed of tree trunks. The piece of furniture was a beautiful creation. The four flat-topped posts were twelve inches across, and could easily hold a vase of flowers. People in St. Louis would pay a fortune for something so sturdy. It would keep her bedroll off the floor. Thank heavens for that! The blackness of the night surrounded them, with the chirp of the crickets the only sound.

Dexter, lying by her chair, sat up and tipped his head, then trotted through the nonexistent wall to the edge of the front porch. He let out a soft growl.

The enormity of where she was filled her. *Montana wilderness. Indians. Wolves.* She looked out into the darkness, trying to see what had riled Dexter, but the light from the lamps made that impossible. Feeling nervous, she walked toward Chance.

Chance placed a gun down, still having one in his holster. Her bedroll was laid out on the thick boards, and several blankets were neatly laid on the floor beside the bed. His rifle was within his reach, too.

"The dog hears something outside."

He stood. "We're outside too, Evie," he said, then chuckled. "But you don't have to worry. Most of the wild creatures have come to terms with the homestead. They cut us a wide berth."

She fretfully fingered a strand of hair. "But—he's growling."

"He's always growling at something. You'll get used to it. Probably a squirrel hunting acorns."

She doubted easing into her new life would be as easy as Chance seemed to think. The streets of St. Louis were noisy, even at night, masking any threatening things that may have been lurking close. She could take the hustle and bustle of the city, but the inky blackness, with silence so vacant it echoed, had her on edge. The clicking of Dexter's nails on the wooden floor made her look over her shoulder. The animal sat by her side. "Guess you're right."

"You having second thoughts?"

His eyes and smile said he didn't think that in the least. He'd been watching her all night, his expressive eyes making her blush at every turn. She'd gone and kissed him in the barn, for goodness' sake! Did he think she was some loose woman just waiting for the sun to set? Well, the night was here, and she had nowhere to go and no one to trust but him. "Of course not."

"Good. You've used the necessary and are all ready to be tucked in."

It was a statement, not a question. She'd had him walk with her out to the outhouse and hold the lantern a few feet away, embarrassing as her request was. She wasn't walking half the distance to the barn after nightfall by herself. The memory of the Victorian's indoor plumbing almost made her sob.

"Yes."

Going to her carpetbag, she rummaged through. She didn't have a clue what she was looking for, she just needed to be grounded by familiar objects from her old life. Oh, how she wished she had Trudy's hanky! Holding the keepsake now would calm her nerves. She closed her eyes and envisioned it in her mind. *Love Never Fails.* When she opened her eyes, Chance was regarding her solemnly.

"Everything all right?"

She nodded. Began unbuttoning the coat.

"You'll need to keep that on. It'll be plenty cold by morning."

Of course! She felt stupid.

The bed was tall. He'd made a small step, and assisted as she clambered in, dragging her long dress. She felt as attractive as a billowing circus tent. It took some doing to get settled without messing up the blankets too much, but with Chance's help she was finally covered and tucked in tight.

With a satisfied smile, he looked down at her. "There. That'll do you fine. Keep you warm."

In six strides, he was through the wall and reached up for the lamp in the kitchen area. Dexter tried to follow him back into the bedroom, but he told the dog to stay put.

Chance lay down on the floor beside her. Bumped around. Got comfortable. "You good up there?"

"Umm."

"Okay, I'm blowing out the lamps."

She heard the scrape of metal on metal. He lifted the first flue, then the sound of his breath. The darkness expanded. The process repeated and the light vanished entirely. As her eyes adjusted to the night, a brilliance of stars filled the sky above.

"Oh, Chance," she whispered, not wanting to mar the beauty with the sound of her voice. "It's so beautiful." She couldn't take her gaze away. Snuggling down into the blankets, she pulled his coat around herself more securely, feeling like a speck of a speck, so tiny she'd be lost if she closed her eyes.

"Yeah, it is," he drawled. "Pretty darn spectacular. I remember being a boy in my bedroll and wondering how the sky could be that big, that bright with stars." A long moment passed. "I still don't know."

"I see what you mean."

"Is this your first time camping?"

"Yes. I've never been out of the house in St. Louis."

"Just wait. If you think this is dark, wake up sometime in the early morning. Around one or two. I've never seen black quite so…black."

Several quiet minutes passed. After the eventful day, it wasn't long before her eyelids drooped. She struggled to keep them open. She wasn't exactly frightened with Chance sleeping nearby, especially with all his guns close by his side. The feeling was more an excited unknown sensation, of how her life had changed, and the wonder of what the future held.

Chapter Eighteen

A *blur of movement caught Evie's eye.*

The inky black body with the sinister long, crinkling legs inched toward her, menacingly.

Her breath jerked, held. Her feet, glued to the floor, felt like immoveable boulders. Before she could blink, the spider skittered and sprang. She screamed.

The thing wriggled under her skirt.

With a sickening awareness, she felt it run across her stomach and crawl across her chest. She groped frantically at the heavy binding keeping her down. She whimpered and moaned. She needed to find it. When she took hold of the foul thing, another shriek ripped from her throat. She gulped air and screamed repeatedly, her head thrashing back and forth as the monster bit her hand.

"Evie, wake up," a voice said urgently. "You're dreaming, darlin'. You're dreaming. It's okay. You're okay."

Violent shivers made her body quake. She felt cold and hot at the same time. The calm voice soothed her fear, distancing her from the panic she felt gripping her insides.

Warm hands gathered her close and rocked her back and forth. Lips, warm and soft, kissed her forehead. "Shhh, you had a nightmare. You're out at the ranch with me. I'd never let anything harm you."

Chance. My husband.

Chance gently scooted her over, making room so he could lie down beside her. He took her in his arms, rested his cheek on her temple, stroked her hair. With one arm, he pulled the thick layers up over them both. Dexter whined, then placed his front paws on the bed, poking his head over to see what was wrong.

Her panic dissolved and she snuggled in close, thankful what she'd just experienced was only a dream. *The* dream. Chance felt good, smelled good, and his heart beating steadily under her ear reinforced her sense of protection. She considered the new feelings that lying so close to her husband produced. She dared to place her hand on his chest, feeling it rise and fall with each breath he took.

"Thank you."

"My pleasure," was his soft reply.

Dexter dropped down to the floor. He slowly wandered off into the dark house.

She fiddled with one of his buttons. "I'm sorry for waking you."

"I've been awake for a while. Just lying here thinking." He pulled her closer. "What were you dreaming about?"

Evie shivered, not able yet to get the words past her lips.

"Let me guess. A spider?"

She nodded. "It's always the same nightmare."

"Well, thank goodness. I thought that scream was you realizing you'd gone and married me. Moved out to the backcountry."

She couldn't stop a small giggle. "No, never that." Feeling bold, she stroked his chest, his nightshirt soft under her fingertips. "When I was only a toddler, a huge black widow crawled into my hair during my nap. I was terrified!

Everyone was terrified, screaming and running around. As hard as it is to believe, I still remember that horrible day!"

Ummm. Chance's chest rumbled. She liked it.

"Look at the stars now, Evie."

Opening her eyes, she tilted her head so she could see the night sky through the open roof. As beautiful and dramatic as the stars had been earlier, their beauty now stole her breath. A vast sea of twinkling lights glittered across the expanse, she couldn't believe how many. "Oh! I don't even have any words to describe how beautiful such a sight is, or the magical feeling I have inside."

"I know what you mean." His arms tightened around her. "You cold?"

"Not anymore."

"Evie, I've been wondering about something."

"Yes?"

"The newspaper advertisement from the agency said I'd need to send a reference letter from our preacher. I thought I'd be asked for that in the first reply I got after I sent in my introduction letter, but that never happened. I just found it a mite strange, the ad saying something was required and then it's never requested."

She swallowed, never taking her gaze from the stars. How she regretted her falsehoods. Things to hide from Chance. She wanted him to know everything about her, and love her no matter what. Even the fact she had been only a maid, not a true mail-order bride. That she'd never known her father, that her mother had borne her in shame. How foolish she'd been not to tell him right away in her letters, the moment she'd stepped from the stage, at dinner her first night in town, or even the day of their wedding. She'd had plenty of opportunities. *But I didn't want him to know. Didn't want to lose him*. Now if he found out, he'd never understand her motivation. He'd think her a cheat and a liar all the days of their lives.

"Evie?"

"I don't know. I guess your introduction was all the matron needed, so she handed your letter on to me." Once the words were out, shame filled her chest.

He stroked her hair. "Would you like me to light the lantern?"

"No," she whispered, thankful for the darkness that kept him from seeing her tears. "The night's too beautiful. I want to enjoy this time for as long as possible." She wished with all her heart she could change the course she'd taken. Her tears made the stars waver and dance before her eyes. She had no one to blame but herself. Her chest heavy with sorrow and guilt, she reached up and discreetly wiped her eyes.

The sound of masculine voices brought Chance striding out of the barn, where he'd scooped each horse a can of oats. The morning sun had just crested the mountaintops. He'd left Evie still asleep, understandably worn out after the night they'd had. She'd about scared the life out of him when she let out the first bloodcurdling shriek. That girl had a hefty fright of spiders. It was no joke. He'd best keep his eyes open and take care of any he saw, before she decided country living wasn't for her.

Chance lifted his hat and scratched his head as Luke, Matthew, Mark, Roady, and Francis rode up into his ranch yard, dismounted, and tied their horses to the hitching rail.

Bringing up the rear was a wagon driven by Lucky. Faith and Amy waved from the seat next to the cook.

Seemed he'd waited too long to take Evie out to the Heart of the Mountains Ranch, so they'd come to her. He glanced over at the house. *Is she awake? Did she hear the commotion, too?* He saw her peering through the beams of the house and frantically trying to calm her wild mass of golden hair. A chuckle rumbled up.

He hurried over to the house as Evie stepped out on the porch, still rumpled from sleep but of composed demeanor.

"What's going on?" Chance asked, striding into the group of horses and men. They all shook hands in greeting.

"You didn't think we'd let you build the place all by yourself, did you? Especially after we found out what happened with the nails," Roady answered, a big grin on his face. He actually laughed and slapped his leg. "You should've seen your face yesterday, Chance, when I said you had your work cut out for you. Man oh man, it was funny. Can you make it again for everyone to see?" He laughed with gusto.

"Hush!" Chance tried to sound aggravated, but that was impossible. These were his friends and they'd come to help. All without his having to ask.

"Morning, Mrs. Holcomb," Matthew McCutcheon said. He touched the brim of his black hat. "You're looking mighty pretty this fine day." The others agreed. "Hope you don't mind us barging in on you like this, but that's how we do things out here in Montana. If Chance has a house to build, we'll do it. Get 'er done in one day." Again the men agreed. "Or as close as we can."

"Thank you," Evie said, a blush creeping up her neck.

When she looked his way, Chance shrugged. "I welcome the help, men. It's good to see you all."

Mark began rolling his sleeves to his elbows, as did the rest of them. Luke helped the women out of the wagon. "Mrs. Holcomb," he called. "I'd like you to meet my wife, Faith, and Mark's wife, Amy." He settled them on the ground. "Matt's wife, her name is Rachel, is home minding our passel of children with the help of our housekeeper, Esperanza, and Esperanza's niece."

By now, the women were up the stairs and gathered around Evie, smiling and giving her hugs.

"We're so happy to finally meet you," Faith said, looking wholesome with her mahogany hair and bright blue dress. "Mr. and Mrs. McCutcheon, as well as Charity, my sister-in-law, are out of town. Hopefully you'll meet them soon."

The sad feeling Chance used to get whenever Faith was close by didn't materialize. He'd been sweet on her for years. The heaviness had lasted so long inside he didn't think the melancholy was ever going to let go of him. But it finally had.

Faith went on, "And we're very sorry for barging in so early in the morning. The men just wouldn't wait no matter how much I begged them. Totally rude to do to newlyweds."

Chance didn't miss Evie's cheeks darken. She looked down from the porch at him and smiled. A silly happiness squeezed his chest. Things *did* have a way of working out for the best.

"But to make up for our charging in uninvited, we brought along enough breakfast and lunch for everyone. And maybe a few meals for later, too. A sort of 'welcome to Y Knot' celebration. Everyone wanted to cook or bake something to send."

As she talked, Francis lifted two sawhorses from the wagon and placed them under the oak tree. Setting a few boards across, they created a table. The women unloaded several wicker baskets, bulging with food, and carried them over.

Evie looked overwhelmed. Chance wanted to help her, but didn't know what to say. "Thank you," she whispered. "I don't know how I can ever thank you."

Lucky limped over. "No need for thanks, missy. Chance is family. And now so are you."

Chance swallowed a lump of emotion. "Where're Billy, Colton, and Adam? I'm surprised they aren't here, too."

"Riding out in a while, after their chores are finished," Luke said. "They were sore put out when we told them their chores came first."

Mark went to the wagon, reaching for a hammer. "Come on, men, get your tools and get to work. This house isn't going to build itself."

Chapter Nineteen

Evie sat on a blanket in the grass, feeling lonely. The sun was long since gone and an evening chill brought gooseflesh to her arms. Every time she thought of her new husband and the warm kisses they'd shared, sparks ignited in her belly, making her heart quicken and her fanciful imagination take wing.

Today was the first time she'd stayed home alone. Over a week ago, when the McCutcheons, Francis, Lucky, Roady, and the women had come out to work, Luke had asked Chance to come over to their ranch to assist with the spring roundup. Chance had wanted her to come along, visit with the women, but she felt the need to prove to her husband that she was capable of doing things on her own.

She'd swept and mopped the floor, plus washed the sheets, some of her underclothing, and several pairs of Chance's thick denim pants. Ashes in the stove had accumulated, so she emptied those too. The fatigue in her arms and legs felt good. The pride she felt in a job well done—work that was sure to please her husband—was her reward.

Finished, and with the day slipping away, she'd ventured out into the front pasture to watch for Chance and the herd. Before long, she'd spot the cattle making their way homeward in the fading light, a sight she was now completely used to, and loved.

Dexter whined beside her, then burrowed down into the grass, the skunk smell gone. "I miss him too, boy," she said, scratching the dog behind the ears. "He'll be home soon."

Surprisingly, she wasn't frightened—at least not too much. She did feel small in the great spectacle of the far-reaching mountains, the huge sky, the vastness of the prairie. Cool puffs of evening air caressed her skin, and she wrapped her arms more tightly around her body. The soft *hoo-hoo-hoo* of a mourning dove calling to its mate soothed her nerves and brought a wistful longing to her soul.

Since coming out to the ranch, Evie hadn't had time to worry about Mrs. Seymour, the marshal, or anything else. Her life had taken on an essence of its own, and the days passed so quickly she wondered how that could be. The house and new friends filled her thoughts, but it was mostly Chance, and the approaching of the wedding-consummation deadline, that made her heart pound with excitement. Was he as anxious as she for them to solidify their union? If he was, he hadn't made that fact known or pressed her in any way.

She turned and looked at the house lit in the warm golden light of the disappearing sun. It was about the prettiest sight she'd ever seen.

Faith and Amy had organized her kitchen with practiced ease, sharing with her reasons why each item belonged where they chose. She showed them the crocheted doily and frying pan that Trudy had given her as wedding gifts. They shared a set of plates and service ware, some sturdy earthen mugs for coffee, and a set of lovely cloth napkins along with some other knickknacks they had brought. A white tablecloth looked charming on the sturdy table Chance had constructed.

"They're extras, just taking up space," Faith had said about the expensive-looking dishes she'd carefully unwrapped. "It'll be nice to have the extra room." After that, she'd placed the set of folded napkins into the built-in pie shelf Roady had crafted on the eastern wall, her spirited expression just daring Evie to object.

Evie's chest warmed thinking about the two women. The day had been wonderful, and the overladen food baskets they'd left behind had kept Chance from learning about her ineptness as a cook.

It was amazing how fast the men had worked. By the end of the day, the house had been finished, including a rock hearth and fireplace. The roof was on, windows and doors set. Taking up the entire far corner of her kitchen was a Glenwood "K" open base range with oven, hot water reservoir on the right side, and a heating oven on top. Chance had the stove stored away in the barn as a surprise. Faith and Amy were smitten with the fancy appliance. They oohed and aahed so much that Luke and Mark had finally taken offense, asking what was wrong with the ovens they had. Every day since, she'd used it to warm the house and the leftovers in speedy comfort and ease.

Dexter jumped to his feet and barked, spotting the cattle coming through the trees and slowly making their way home.

"Shhh, boy," she said, after he barked several times. "No need alerting every living creature within a mile." She'd heard the stories about Indians, the Cheyenne of Montana and Wyoming. Most were on reservations, but some still lived hidden away in the mountains, unwilling to submit and be kept by the white man. Chance had assured her several times that there weren't any troublemakers in this part of the country. None at least that he knew about.

As she watched the herd making its way up the trail, she worried how she was going to learn how to bake and cook. She wanted desperately to make Chance proud of her. She especially longed to make him a birthday cake, one like Mrs. Klinkner had been baking the day of her visit. His birthday would be here before she knew it. She needed to find a way to get over to Ina's house.

A long whistle brought Dexter around. Before she knew what he was up to, the dog bolted for the road where she saw Chance loping in her direction. She stood, adjusting the folds of her skirt. A longing deep inside pulled at her thoughts, her heart. She ached to be one with him, and yet the thought frightened her, too.

He reined up and dismounted. "Evie."

All of a sudden, the cat had her tongue, her nerve, and everything else.

He removed his hat and pushed back his hair, rolling his shoulders as if to relieve tension. "If I weren't so dirty, I'd give you a hug."

Grime covered his leather chaps. His shirt was dusty. Boston's head drooped, his neck and hips smelling of warm, sweaty horseflesh. "I can't remember a longer day. I'm especially glad now you weren't there."

His eyes said he wanted her. He took a small step forward, then bent down and brushed her lips briefly. Had he missed her as she had him? A smile played around his mouth. "How are you? Your day went well?"

"Yes. Dexter kept me company the whole time." At the mention of his name, the dog tipped his head and wagged his tail.

Chance picked up her blanket from the ground and tossed it over his saddle, then started toward the ranch house.

"That's good. After I was finished at the McCutcheons I went into town, picked up a few things. Fancy Aubrey said to tell you hello." He smiled again. "As well as Ina. She asked about you, wants me to bring you for a visit." He paused, looking out at the pasture where she'd been waiting for him. "What'ar you doing way out here in the grass? I'm surprised."

She pointed out toward the cattle coming in their single line, all the while wondering where he'd seen Fancy. "Waiting for them to come home. Just felt quiet without you."

"No spiders in the grass?"

She shook her head. "That's why I brought the blanket."

He slung his arm over her shoulders as they walked, keeping his clothes from touching her dress. So natural, it was as if they'd been man and wife for years.

"I have something for you."

When she glanced up, he took a letter from his pocket. "Arrived yesterday at the store. From your friend in St. Louis."

"Trudy! So soon!"

She took the letter and lovingly turned the envelope over, examining every inch.

"Aren't you going to open it?"

She shrugged.

"Women," he stated, and then chuckled.

They were in front of the house, and she was torn by the need to run inside and read the letter, or walk to the barn and watch him unsaddle his horse. He must have seen her indecision.

"You go on inside while I take care of Boston. I'll be in shortly. After supper, we'll walk out and check to see if there were any more calves born today."

"You sure?" She hesitated. She'd spent time watching him care for the stock. He seemed to enjoy her company. "I've gotten pretty friendly with the horses in the paddock. Skip lets me stroke his nose from my side of the fence and Roan comes when I call." She glanced over to find the two horses looking expectantly their way.

"Go on now before I change my mind." He gestured to the envelope she had clutched next to her heart. "I can see this means a lot to you."

Nodding, she turned, then gathered her dress.

"Oh, would you mind heating some water on the stove? I'm in desperate need of a bath."

"I've already done that. It's ready when you are."

At his astonished look, she hurried up the steps and into the warm house, which smelled of the last of the stew from Faith and Amy that was warming on the stove. Before opening the letter, she stoked the fire and glanced around, making sure everything was perfect. She lit the lantern in the middle of the table, sending a cheery light into the room.

How easy a job to keep this place tidy. So different from Mrs. Seymour's gigantic Victorian, and only the two of them to pick up after. She hurried to the bedroom, making sure she'd tucked away her feather duster. Every time she used it, she thought of Mrs. Seymour and felt a twinge of sadness.

Satisfied with everything, she lowered herself into a kitchen chair. With trembling hands, she carefully opened the envelope.

Chapter Twenty

Chance ambled to the barn, Dexter at his heels and his tired horse lagging behind. He'd left at sunrise and they'd worked hard all day. Exhaustion made his step slow, and his eyes droop. Thankfully, after leaving McCutcheons', he'd made good time into Y Knot just as Mr. Lichtenstein was turning the Open sign, barely making it to pick up Evie's letter. He was glad he could do that one small thing for her.

Visions of Evie scrubbing his wet back with a soft-bristled brush brought a wistful smile to his face. There was a possibility, albeit small, that if he asked nicely, she'd help with his bath. All sorts of feelings and ideas tumbled around when he thought of his new wife. He'd spotted her in the grass right away, looking tiny against the backdrop of the distant mountain range. Was she homesick? How long before she missed the hustle and bustle of St. Louis? He didn't like to think about her leaving.

His stomach tightened painfully. He'd taken the good-natured ribbing from the ranch hands today, no less than one would expect after just getting hitched. Nevertheless, the jokes about his beautiful wife, having enough of living with a country bumpkin and hightailing it back to the city had unknowingly hit their mark. Evie was educated, refined, came from money. What the heck was she doing with him, alone, out in the Montana wild land, instead of living a life of ease in the city? It just didn't make sense.

He lit a lantern, then went about unsaddling and rubbing down his mount. The other horses nickered from the outside paddock in hopes of getting a handout.

Evie seemed happy to see him. She didn't act as if she regretted her decision—but then, his mother hadn't given them any clue, either, before packing up and leaving them all behind.

With his horse turned out, Chance plunked down on the bench and lowered his head into his hands. He should have thought this through longer before sending for a city girl. Even if she had taken a fancy to him, that might not be enough to keep her here, not when the weather turned and the going got rough. If he were honest with himself, the reason he'd wanted her to come along today was to make sure she wouldn't pack her bag and leave. He'd been so relieved when he'd spotted her in the grass…shaken, too, at how worked up he'd let himself get. On his way home, he'd pushed his horse harder than he should.

Lifting his head, he hefted the saddlebag slumped next to him on the bench into his lap, and unbuckled the keep. As well as the letter from her friend, he'd picked up a few things at the store that might make life a little easier for her. Boy-sized store-made britches, along with a cotton shirt. He'd seen her struggle with the yards of fabric of her brown dress, the garment she'd worn every day since arriving. He wouldn't want to work in one of those. Besides, Charity McCutcheon had been wearing pants for years, even into town at times. If Luke's little sister didn't care what people thought, Evie shouldn't, either. She might put up a fuss at first, but when she got used to them, and realized how easy they made her chores, she'd see the light.

Ina Klinkner and Hayden had been in the store, too. Hayden had watched as he'd set items for Evie on the counter. Had the gall to ask about her, and tell him they'd met at his house. Evie hadn't mentioned that when she'd told him about going to the Klinkners. Why not? Jealousy gnawed at him. The light shining from Hayden's eyes about drove him wild, that along with his know-it-all expression while speaking about her. *All too many questions about my wife for propriety. Just you try it, Klinkner. I'd welcome a go-round with you.*

He sighed, knowing he was being mulish, then looked over the other trinkets he'd picked up for Evie, wondering if he was being a dang fool. What did he have to offer someone like her? Seriously. That woman, Mrs. Seymour, must have been tipsy when she matched the two of them together.

Chance removed his hat, swabbed his face with his shirtsleeve, then proceeded to tinker with the felt brim. Evie was refined where he was coarse. She was educated where he'd only completed his sixth year. She was used to culture and society, where he valued the expanse of the blue sky and company of hawks and cattle, even as much as another would treasure a precious diamond. He and Evie were like oil and water—not made for mixing. Maybe Ernie, back home, was better suited to her. He shook his head, then looked at the faithful friend sitting at his feet. "What say you, Dex? Is my exhaustion trying to trip me up? You think she'll stick around?"

The dog, aware he was being addressed, whined earnestly and laid his head on Chance's thigh. His sorrowful dark brown eyes said it all.

"Yeah, I was afraid of that." He stroked Dexter's warm neck, then settled his hat on his head. Standing, he corralled his nagging doubts. "My thoughts exactly."

Looking at the words on the cream-colored paper, Evie imagined Trudy's loving smile. St. Louis didn't feel quite so far away.

> *Dear Evie,*
>
> *It was with great relief and thankfulness that I read your letter telling me you had arrived safely in Y Knot and that your Chance seems everything you had hoped. I must admit to some envy about the "devilishly handsome" description, and hope I will be able to give a similar description of my Seth. However, I have told myself to adopt a more practical frame of mind. He is what he is, and I will have to live with it—or rather him.*

Pausing a moment, Evie closed her eyes, recalling the day she had stepped off the stage in Y Knot and encountered Chance for the very first time. Her breath caught, unable to believe how blessed she'd been.

> *Although, my dear friend, I am going to take you to task for not giving me more description. I want to know what Chance looks like and how you find Y Knot. Have you met his family and friends, and what do you think of them? I cannot wait to hear about your home. Do not fail to omit any details.*

Evie giggled. That was Trudy. Always straight to the point.

> *My father's wedding takes place in one week. His fiancée has already packed up most of her possessions, and some of them have made their way into our house. When I am not at the agency, I am sorting through my family's paraphernalia and choosing which to*

take with me. My father is most generous. You should see the wooden crates stacked in the parlor!

A quick glance around the sparsely furnished living room reminded Evie of the few things, besides herself, that she had brought into this union with Chance. Trudy had numerous crates. Boxes of knickknacks. Stacks of trimmings and frills. Everything to make a home beautiful and inviting. Oh, how lacking she'd been in her marriage! A frying pan, a feather duster, a manners manual, the clothes on her back. Poor Chance. He would've been better off with another of the brides. Maybe Heather with her thick black hair and quick sense of humor? Kathryn, with her rich family, easy smile, and gift for writing poetry? What about Darcy Russell and Angelina Napolitano? All most certainly good choices. Prudence? *No!* She wouldn't consider that mean-spirited, sassy-mouthed agitator for her worst enemy, let alone her darling Chance. That she-cat wasn't a match for anyone!

Evie pushed away her doubts, insecurities, and painful thoughts. Squaring her shoulders, she glanced at the pretty Home Sweet Home keepsake she'd given Chance their first night; the gift now hung over the hearth. Her husband, for better or for worse, was going to be in the house in just a few minutes. She mustn't greet him with a frown on her face or sadness in her eyes. She'd do everything in her power to make him happy. Mrs. Seymour's book said a happy, cheerful spirit was what all men loved.

She returned her focus to the letter, wanting to finish before Chance stepped through the door.

I am sure by the time you receive my letter, you will have married and be living in wedded bliss. Of course, you will share the details with your dear friend! I will write you again when I reach Sweetwater Springs and meet my Seth.

Your fellow mail-order bride and friend,
Trudy Bauer

Finished, Evie inhaled a deep breath of the warm, aromatic air and sat motionless in the quiet room, the letter forgotten in her hands. A moment passed. She wished the letter were twice as long. She wished Trudy had mentioned Mrs. Seymour and what her reaction was when she found her gone. She thought of Trudy's hanky and the words Trudy's mother had stitched so thoughtfully. *Love Never Fails.* She hoped it was true.

She recognized the feeling filling her heart as love. Love for a man she'd just met and, in all honesty, hardly knew. Did he return that feeling? He'd never said so. But then, she hadn't expressed her own feelings, either. Maybe the time had arrived. His eyes seemed to say he did. What if he knew about her deception? How would he look at her then? Too many questions she didn't have the answers for. She'd answer Trudy's letter tonight, then hopefully post it tomorrow. The sound of Chance's footsteps on the steps outside chased all her fears away.

Chapter Twenty-One

Chance drew the buckboard to a halt in front of Ina Klinkner's house. This morning, in preparation for her visit with the mill owner's wife, Evie had primped and fussed so long—doing this, that, and whatever—that he had been driven to distraction. Her cheerful humming had penetrated the closed bedroom door, prompting him to chomp the inside of his cheek several times as he ate his porridge. When she'd finally emerged, she'd told him she was too excited to sit down with him, or eat a thing.

His patience stretched to the limit, he set the brake with a jerk, then glanced at her. She looked charming in her yellow dress and upswept hair. Was this all for Hayden's benefit? Had she taken a fancy to him the other day?

"Here we are," he said, his voice low and even. He tied the reins to the brake, jumped to the ground and went around to help her. When she placed her hands on his shoulders, he suddenly had to fight the urge to pull her close. He trained his gaze away from her lovely-looking lips, tamping down the desire to capture them with his own.

"Thank you so much, Chance, for allowing me this day with Mrs. Klinkner. Driving me all the way—"

"No problem," he said, cutting her off.

Her brows pulled together.

Good. Maybe she needed to realize Hayden was a schmuck.

"So you'll be back around five?" she asked tentatively.

"That's what we decided, isn't it?"

Even though he felt justified, speaking to her so crossly didn't feel right. He glanced across the street to the mill, where steam billowed and the sound of the saw cutting wood filled the air. He clenched his teeth and looked away.

"If you'd rather I not go, I can certainly do that. This idea isn't set in stone."

Oh, sure. Now that she was *here* she wanted to go with him—*right.*

"No. We'll stick to our plan. I'll post this letter in town." He patted his front shirt pocket. "Then go back out to the ranch and do my ranching, then come back and fetch you home later. Not before five, though, as you've requested."

It hurt him to be so curt with her, yet a part of him wanted her to feel as much pain as he had the night before, when she'd made her initial request. After he'd bathed and eaten, they'd walked out in the pasture hand in hand to check on the cattle. Moonlight all around. Peaceful herd, the cattle calm and resting. No new calves, just the two they already had, frolicking around their mamas in the evening air. The hoot of an owl and the soft call of a mourning dove was music to further set the scene. A lush, cool breeze enveloped them and he snuggled Evie closer to his side. The huge flower moon suspended on the treetops. The twinkle of early evening stars, fairy dust all around.

Everything was perfect. The rightness of his decision to marry Evie moved his soul. Made him whole. Made him long for the children they would bring forth to enrich their lives and be their legacy.

Just as he'd opened his mouth to share what was in his heart, tell her he'd fallen deeply and madly in love with her, she'd sprung the idea on him. Brought up the subject of going into Y Knot today. *To the Klinkners.* To see Ina—or did she really mean *Hayden?* That burr under his saddle was at the mill every day. Chance had never been out there when Hayden wasn't working. Luke had given the scoundrel his final warning, last Christmas, about his open flirtation with Faith. Chance had seen Hayden in action too many times to feel comfortable with Evie's spending the day here. What made the situation worse was *Evie* doing the asking, not Klinkner. Why hadn't she told him about meeting Hayden the first time? Did she have something to hide?

I'd love some time with Ina, if I could. Do you think it would be possible for me to spend the day with her tomorrow?

After her request, the beauty of the evening had evaporated in a sizzling pop. Was she pining to see Hayden again? When he'd asked her about him—or, rather, why exactly she wanted to go to the Klinkners'—her face had turned a rosy pink and she'd sputtered for something to say.

He felt foolish now, thinking love could grow between them so quickly. Had he expressed that notion, she'd have thought him a dolt. It was obvious she missed life in a town—friends, society—*all the things Hayden could give her.* The joy of the small gifts he had purchased for her, including the clothes, turned into humiliation. He'd kept them in his saddlebag, angry with himself for spending the money and wasting time at the store trying to figure out what would please her most.

As if on cue, Hayden appeared, striding around the corner of the mill. He smiled. Waved. "Mornin', Chance, Mrs.

Holcomb," he called. He took off his hat and ran his sleeve across his sweaty brow, giving Evie a show of his long-johns-clad chest. Evie gave a small, discreet wave and had the decency not to reply.

She looked up searchingly into Chance's face. "All right," she said finally. "If you're sure you don't mind picking me up later. I'll just go see if today is good for her. Do you mind waiting?"

"'Course not."

Before Evie got to the porch, the door opened. A delighted smile flashed across the older woman's face when she saw Evie and she promptly enfolded his wife into a hug. They talked. Ina glanced his way. He was almost sure Evie dropped her voice so he couldn't hear what she was saying. What were they cooking up, anyway? Did Ina already know she was coming? Did the woman want Evie as a daughter-in-law? The idea was crazy, he knew even as he thought it, but then again he wouldn't put anything past Hayden. And nothing had been consummated. He hadn't taken her as his wife, not in that way. What were the rules of the law? Certainly their vows were binding regardless, weren't they?

The women withdrew their fluffy heads from the huddle. "Chance," Ina called. "Would you like to come in for a cup of coffee? It's fresh."

"No, thank you, ma'am, I have lots of work to do," he replied, climbing into the wagon and picking up his reins. Despite the coolness of the morning, a warm sheen broke out on his forehead. "I'll be back—later."

Evie waved. Her cheery smile contradicted the way her brows pulled down worriedly on her forehead. The women watched as he flicked the reins over the horses' backs and turned the wagon. They remained standing, waving, for a good few moments until he was at the bend in the road. One last glance showed them back together, bursting into giggles, and then hurrying through the door.

"Why, I'd be honored to teach you how to bake a cake, dear," Mrs. Klinkner said, closing the front door with a click. "It'll be fun. I'm waiting for the day I have a daughter-in-law or granddaughter to share my recipes with." Her pleased face all but glowed. "But let's not tarry. We have lots to do and only a few hours to do it. Come along. It takes finesse to get cake just right and the icing light and fluffy." She scurried away.

Evie followed behind, worrying what had come over Chance. Ever since last night, he'd been acting strange. Detached. Cold. Maybe even angry—but how could that be? She didn't have the foggiest idea why. She'd fed him the leftovers again last night, then this morning had managed to boil up some hot cereal. Mrs. Seymour's book said grumpy men were the result of empty bellies. Was that it—the food wasn't satisfactory? Or could his crankiness have something to do with his seeing Fancy Aubrey yesterday? He hadn't given her many details except that he'd seen her on the boardwalk in town and she'd asked him to tell her hello.

A niggle of suspicion sprouted, but she quickly pushed the feeling away. No. Fancy wouldn't do that. *Fancy is my friend. Nevertheless, Fancy herself said she went after other women's husbands, didn't she? Would she go after Chance?* Angry with herself for even entertaining such an idea, she turned her thoughts away from Fancy and Chance. She'd not conjure up something out of nothing.

But something *was* wrong. Was he miffed over the marriage's waiting stipulation? Feeling lonely? There could be lots of things. When she'd asked, he'd just frowned and looked away.

She followed Mrs. Klinkner across the parlor and hurried into the homey kitchen she remembered so well.

"I can't tell you what this means to me, Mrs. Klinkner," Evie said softly, still worried about Chance and their quiet ride into town.

The older woman placed her hands on her hips. "I *insist* you call me Ina. Mrs. Klinkner sounds so formal. Nothing formal about baking a cake."

Evie smiled. "All right then, Ina. Do you think I'll be able to learn to bake and cook in one day? Chance's birthday is on the twenty-seventh, and I have my heart set on baking him a cake."

"Well, we have to start somewhere, and God willing, we can. First, keep in mind you'll need a good four inches of coals to have your oven hot enough to bake. Also, don't skimp on the warm-up time. Allow an hour and a half if your stove is cold and not a minute less. I've already been cooking this morning so we won't have to wait."

Ina rummaged through a drawer, extracted a wrinkled yellow apron, and handed it to Evie. "Here, put this on. We don't want to soil your pretty yellow dress."

She did as instructed.

Ina riffled through her recipe box. "Do you have any cake pans or baking utensils?"

"One pan my girlfriend gave me. Nothing else except what Chance has, which isn't much. I have to admit, Ina...I'm a horrible cook. If it weren't for the food Faith and Amy

McCutcheon brought out the other day, and the meals Chance has prepared himself, we'd pretty much starve."

Ina tsk-tsked and gave her a dubious look. "I'll get you in that kitchen baking and cooking faster than you can sing 'Jimmy Cracked Corn'! And I'll lend you my things when the time comes. Also, when we get the cake in the oven"—she pulled out a dog-eared, food-splotched card and placed it on the drainboard—"I'll give you a few easy recipes to take home, but not before we go over them. You'll see. Cooking isn't hard. Just takes a little imagination. And determination."

Evie doubted cooking could be that easy. She could keep the house perfectly, remove the toughest of stains on a blouse, and wax a floor beyond tomorrow—but bake a cake? She might as well try to fly to the moon. Doubtfully, she glanced at the recipe sitting on the counter top.

Chocolate Mashed Potato Cake.

Mashed potatoes?

That didn't sound enticing, but Evie held off voicing her opinion. Ina knew better and she'd not look a gift horse in the mouth.

"I can see the questions in your eyes. I picked this recipe because it's basically a foolproof formula—not calling you a fool, of course, dear. I got it last year from Miss Langford, Y Knot's schoolteacher. I'm sure you'll be able to accomplish this at home without my help and simply dazzle your new husband. No one would ever guess the ingredients unless you told them, which I advise you not to do. The mashed potatoes will keep the cake from falling."

She pulled out the bottom drawer of a small freestanding cabinet and extracted three large brown spuds and handed them to Evie. "First, we'll get these cooking. Have you ever prepared mashed potatoes before?"

Evie's face heated.

Ina's eyes opened wide. "Well, take these to the sink and rinse them off, for starters."

When Evie was finished, Ina placed a light, metal object in her hands. "Now peel. I'm putting on a pot of water—always start that first. When you're done peeling, you'll dice up the potatoes and put them in the water. They won't take long to cook."

It took some doing, but Evie managed to get the hang of the potato peeler. That task accomplished, she next creamed two-thirds of a cup of butter with two cups of sugar, just as Ina directed, until the slippery mass was fluffy and white. Her arm ached from whipping, and the long wooden spoon was cumbersome. She tried to keep up the pace Ina wanted, but that was difficult.

Next, she ruined three perfectly good eggs trying to separate the yolks from the whites. The process—dumping the yolk from half shell to half shell to let the white drip away—was tricky and slimy and totally unappealing. Gooey clumps of white stuff jiggled around in the clear, uncooked egg, making her queasy. When she finally had four separated yolks without any shells, all completed to Ina's liking, she beat them into her mixture.

With a fork, she tested the spuds. They were soft, as Ina said they should be. Draining the water and pressing out all the lumps, she added one cup of the still hot mashed potatoes to the egg mixture, wondering how this was all going to turn out.

To her surprise, she realized that somewhere during the process she'd begun to relax and enjoy herself. Maybe cooking wouldn't be so hard after all!

Ina made them both a cup of tea while keeping a sharp eye on Evie to make sure she didn't do anything wrong or hurt herself. The older woman kept her laughing with amusing stories of when she was young and first in love with Norman.

"Now, blend in one teaspoon of vanilla and one-half cup of this unsweetened cocoa. When you're finished, set it to the side."

Evie did as Ina instructed. Task accomplished, she took the end of her apron and wiped at her moist brow, just as the door opened and footsteps sounded in the entry.

Chapter Twenty-Two

Still agitated, Chance crossed Main Street, his wagon jangling and rattling as he pulled his team to a halt in front of the livery. Every possible situation of why Evie wanted to spend the day with Ina bounced around in his mind until his head hurt. With each passing moment, his jealousy grew until it felt like a veritable demon writhing inside him. Distractedly, he hopped out of the buckboard and strode into the big barn as if he owned the place. A chicken, frightened by his abrupt entry, squawked loudly and flew out the window. Chance let his eyes adjust to the dim interior.

"Hello?" June called from the hayloft.

"Yeah, it's Chance."

"What are you doing to my chickens?"

"Nothing."

"Be nice or they won't lay a thing."

When he didn't answer, she looked down. A small smile played around her lips. "Haven't seen much of you lately. What brings you around now?"

That was a heck of a good question. Why was he here? He'd just needed somewhere to go, someone to talk to. He was way out of his element with Evie and this whole situation and didn't know how to proceed. Was he justified in his anger, or was he making a mountain out of a molehill? He didn't know. One moment he thought he knew, and the next he was hopelessly mixed up—and furious.

June was a woman. Maybe she'd have some insight into what he should do, or whether there even was a problem in the first place.

"My right front wheel on the buckboard has been giving me trouble. Wondered if you had any extras around I might buy." *Buy! You're stretched thin enough.*

"Funny, you never mentioned that before."

She was almost down the ladder, and he wondered what she would say when she saw the wheel was perfectly fine. Without wasting a step, she passed him by and started for the tall twin doors.

"Wait!"

She turned around and gave him a questioning look. "Just what's going on, Holcomb? I've never seen you so out of sorts. You look like you just lost your best friend." She glanced around. "By the way, where is Dexter anyway?"

It was no use. He was no good at either fibbing or acting. He'd best get to the point. "My wheel is fine, actually."

Her brows peaked up. "You been sitting in the sun too long?"

He shrugged.

She waited.

"Guess I just needed a friendly face, someone to talk with."

She walked toward him slowly, then stopped. "This doesn't have anything to do with that fancy new wife of yours, does it? The one that just arrived—what?—thirteen days ago?"

He shrugged, feeling like the biggest fool on earth. "Maybe."

June took him by the arm and propelled him over by her small desk, dusted off the top of a chair and pushed him down with a plunk.

Hayden Klinkner stood in the doorway to the kitchen. His wide shoulders filled the space. His body-hugging shirt accentuated his muscular chest, strong arms and slender hips. When Evie realized she was staring, she jerked her gaze away, but not before she saw him smile.

"Hayden? Do you need something?" Ina set her teacup into its saucer.

He strode across the room, took a glass from the cupboard, and worked the pump. "Just came in for a glass of water."

"Oh—did the bucket in the stream get loose and float away again?"

He turned around and smiled. "No. Just needed a break."

The tilt of her chin said Ina knew exactly why her son was here. "Mrs. Holcomb is busy. Don't come in here to tease. I know you better than you know yourself."

Evie wished she didn't know that look in his eyes. He was a scoundrel, the kind of man Mrs. Seymour always warned her girls against. "They'll flirt with you, and if you're not careful, use you, and leave your reputation in tatters. Avoid a rogue at all costs."

She brushed at her spotted apron, trying to will her cheeks from turning pink. What was he thinking when he looked at her like that?

Hayden chuckled, then drank down his water in three long swallows. On his way out the door, he stopped and looked into the bowl on the drain board. He started to stick his finger in, but Ina smacked him away with a wooden spoon. "Out with you! That is not yours!"

He chuckled again and tossed Evie one more charming smile before leaving.

Ina plunked her hands on her hips and watched until he was out of sight. "I swear! If I don't get him married off soon, one of the men in Y Knot is going to—to do I don't know what to him, but it's bound to be bad. I hate to say that, but it's true. He goes around making a pest of himself and angering all the husbands. If he would only find the right girl and settle down. Give Norman and me a couple of grandbabies to bounce on our knees. To coddle. To spoil." She shrugged. "I'm sorry if he embarrassed you."

"No, it's all right." Evie pulled herself together, trying to remember what she was supposed to be doing next. She pushed some hair out of her face with the back of her hand, then looked around.

Mrs. Klinkner watched her a moment and then a light flickered in her eyes. "Are there others like *you*, Evie?" At Evie's confused look she added, "I mean, other nice, charming young women at the mail-order brides agency where Chance found you? Others wanting to come west? Marry fine, upstanding young men? Perhaps you know someone. Hayden…" She walked to the window, looking out at the flowering hyacinth.

"Ina?"

"Oh, never mind, dear. It's just a silly dream. Now, where were we?"

Ina's flushed face gave Evie the distinct impression she was cooking something up besides cake.

"Let's see, yes," the older woman said. "I remember now. In a separate bowl, you'll need to sift together two cups of flour, three pinches of salt, two teaspoons of baking powder, and one teaspoon each of cinnamon and cloves." She helped Evie measure and spoon the ingredients into the sifter without too much mess. "Now sift. It's not hard."

Ina was right. Evie loved sifting. The gliding motion was easy and fun. Much more pleasant than beating butter until she thought her arm would come off her shoulder. The soft particles of mixture floating to the bottom of the bowl reminded her of Christmastime in St. Louis. St. Louis reminded her of Trudy, and Trudy reminded her of Mrs. Seymour—and the agency, and how she'd left there without a good-bye. That still hurt. It wasn't something she was proud of. Her heart thumped, and she blinked away her somber mood.

"Is something wrong, dear?"

Evie looked over, unaware that she'd stopped sifting only to stare at the flour in the bottom of the bowl. She shook her head. "Just thinking about St. Louis and my friends there."

Ina came over and put a warm hand on Evie's arm. "Must be difficult leaving everyone you love behind to venture so far away and marry a man you don't even know. If there's anything you need, or want to talk about, you know you can come to me. I've always liked Chance Holcomb. He's smart and honest, two qualities that go a long way here in Montana." For a moment, she looked over, as if she could see through the walls to the mill across the road where her son was at work. "Sincere, too." Her smile wobbled and she shrugged.

Evie nodded, taking Ina's words to heart. "Thank you so much. That means more to me than you could know."

"Well, I mean every bit of it." She patted Evie's arm a few times, then picked up the recipe card and gave it a quick read. "Fine, then. Now, mix the dry ingredients with the butter mixture while you add in a cup of milk. I'll go get that now."

Ina disappeared to a small room outside her kitchen door and came back with a pitcher of milk. She measured a cup and poured a small amount on the batter. "Not too much at once. Go ahead and stir until I tell you to stop."

Back on task, Evie was starting to realize that making a cake was no little thing. They'd been working for at least forty-five minutes and the confection still wasn't in the oven. And what a mess. It would take another hour to get the kitchen back into shape. Ina must have noticed what she was thinking. "Don't worry, honey. As you practice, you'll learn it's best to clean up as you go. It'll get easier."

Evie couldn't hold back a soft laugh. "I hope so. This has certainly been an undertaking." Finished with the milk, and making sure there were no lumps or bumps in the batter, she thought she was finished.

"We're not quite done yet. Remember the four egg whites? You still need to beat them until they're stiff and form into little peaks. It takes a strong arm." She handed Evie a small wire whisk.

Twenty minutes later, the cake was finally in the oven. Evie sank onto a kitchen chair, tired but feeling triumphant. "That was more fun than I'd expected."

"Yes. And like I said, it'll get easier too. I do, however insist that we have another day just like this. Let's say a week from today. That will give you some time to practice and by then I'm sure you'll have lots of questions, too."

Ina brought to the table two new cups of steaming peppermint tea and a plate of cookies. Evie took one and bit into it hungrily. The women sat then in companionable silence for a few minutes, enjoying the refreshment.

"I'll get your kitchen cleaned up right away, Ina, as soon as we finish our tea," Evie said at last.

Ina set her cup into its saucer with a clatter. "But, Evie," she chided gently. "We still have so much we could do. I have ingredients and the volition to teach you a creamy parsnip soup and sorghum bread. After that, I thought we'd make a slaw and maybe a potato salad. Remember, many of the things I teach you today can be used with other foods. You have to be inventive. Have fun with cooking. Experiment."

Chapter Twenty-Three

All doubts Evie might have had that Chance was circling something unpleasant were confirmed when she saw his grumpy face where he stood on Ina's doorstep at five o'clock sharp. His mouth was a straight, hard line, his eyes, unreadable.

Was he sorry he married her? Was that it? Had everything happened too fast for his liking? Perhaps he was making his feelings known so she'd take the stage out of Y Knot and out of his life. He'd barely acknowledged her, just waited with his hat in his hands while she gathered her things.

"How was your day," she said, hoping to draw him into conversation as they walked to the buckboard. His mumbled response only heightened her anxiety. They drove through town without a single word between them, and still had a good half-hour-long ride ahead. She wrapped the blanket he'd brought along for her more securely around her shoulders and hoped he'd soften up.

"The cattle?" she tried again softly, letting the sway of the wagon ease her mind.

"Actually, it was good."

She smiled, and a moment of relief washed through her. "Were there any more babies born today?"

"Yep. Two. Both bulls."

"Oh." She remembered his saying he'd prefer heifers over bull calves. Something about growing the herd faster. "Would girls have been better?"

He looked over at her, as if trying to decide if she were being sincere. An uncharacteristic frown drew down the corners of his lips. Why would he do that? Of course she'd be interested in what her husband did, thought, dreamed. Feeling a stab of irritation, she straightened and held his gaze, refusing to let him off the hook. "Well? Didn't you tell me that the other day? Heifers were preferable?"

He cleared his throat and looked straight ahead. "Sure. I said that. But if these two grow up with the conformation I think they will, I should be able to sell them for a fair amount. Other ranchers will be interested when they see the quality of *my* beef."

She thought of her heartfelt efforts today, all to please him, take care of him. His coldness fired her temper. "*Your* beef? Don't you mean *our* beef?"

He shrugged evasively. "I guess. What's mine is yours if you want to nitpick," he drawled, glancing out to the prairie, away from her. "Whatever."

Why, the big, fat, unfeeling ox! He didn't even have the courtesy to look at her. Plus his uninterested mollifying tone ruffled her ire even more.

Didn't he have a thought to her feelings? She had hopes and dreams, too! This wasn't the man who'd met her at the stage with a torrent of beautiful words, supped with her by candlelight, held her close in the darkness of night under a canopy of twinkling stars while calming her fears.

No! This Chance Holcomb was a stranger to her, coarse, closed-minded, and infuriating. He couldn't care less if her heart were breaking. If she jumped out of the wagon this moment, he probably wouldn't even notice. She'd worked her fingers to the bone today, trying to learn how to cook, just to please him. She'd burned her arm, sliced a finger, and got egg in her hair. And for what? All so she could bake a stupid cake for his stupid birthday!

Knowing it was childish, she glanced his way and stuck out her tongue, not that he'd notice; his gaze was glued straight ahead. She'd show him. Taking a deep, calming breath, she replied sweetly, "I'm so happy to hear that, Chance. When the time comes when I want to buy the piano I've always dreamed of owning, I'll just sell off an acre or two of land. Especially now that I know you won't mind. I know exactly where to put it in *my* house. Right in front of *my* picture window."

His mouth dropped open. He looked about to say something, but didn't, slapping the reins over the horses' backs. The wagon jerked forward as the surprised horses picked up their pace.

Evie gripped the side rail to keep from being bounced out. Remorse for her outlandish behavior had filled her the moment she'd closed her mouth. *What am I doing? We're not children. There's a lot at stake.* From the time she was a child, her mama had said there wasn't anything that couldn't be fixed with a simple conversation. She'd best remember that and not be pulled into mirroring Chance's immature behavior. She might even have to eat a little crow.

"Chance?" she asked, looking at his angry profile. "What's wrong? Please tell me."

He glanced at her, his expression unreadable, but seemed to be mulling over his response. He turned back to the road. "Nothing. Nothing at all."

In misery, she turned her face away, unable to look at him for another moment. What had happened? Why was he rejecting her? And why had she let her temper get the better of her to make such a senseless, juvenile statement? She didn't even play the piano, let alone dream about owning one.

Her eyes filled, and she set her jaw to keep from crying. All she wanted to do was make him happy! And she was doing everything but. They were married. Man and wife. She had to try to make things right, or else…or else what?

"My day was lovely," she said haltingly, trying to keep her voice steady. "I had the nicest time with Ina and her family. I really like them, admire them. They're good people." There. That was about the safest ground she could tread. After a moment, and the sounds of the evening being her only response, she ventured a look in his direction, hoping he'd turn his head and meet her halfway. He did, all right, but with a look so cold ice crystals formed on her heart. Then he turned forward again. After that, a chiseled rock couldn't have been more unresponsive as he sat silently on the rocking buckboard seat.

Chance searched his recollection for what June had told him to try: Don't jump to conclusions. Things may not be what they seem. Give in. Laugh. Say you're sorry. Smile. Tell her she's pretty. Give her the benefit of the doubt. Talk things out.

Talk? Hell! He couldn't even think. Especially when she so brazenly threw Hayden in his face, all but proclaiming her admiration and respect for the man. Great waves of energy pulled at his chest, making his heart thwack against his ribs so hard he expected her to ask what the commotion was. This had been about the longest day of his life, waiting for five o'clock to roll around. Perdition, for sure.

At the turnoff, he guided the team off the main road and onto the quarter-mile lane that crossed his front pasture and led to the house. Halfway there he spotted Dexter, apparently hearing their approach and sprinting through the grass to greet them. His wife hadn't said a thing since her last proclamation of love for the Klinkner family.

"Whoa." He pulled up in front of the house in silence and set the brake, wondering how they were going to cohabitate without acknowledging each other. He got out and, not knowing what else to do, went slowly around the wagon to her side, intending to help her down. He was just a cowboy. What the heck did she expect of him, anyway?

There she sat wrapped in the blanket, her chin jutting out and her eyes straight ahead. He waited. Surely, she wasn't going to sit there all night. Did she want an apology? What would he apologize for? Driving her into Y Knot and picking her up again?

"Evie."

When she didn't move or speak, he reached down and patted Dexter's head. "Hey there, Dex. How you doin', boy?" The dog's happy display of affection did little to lighten his mood. He waited with the chirping crickets and the rustle of soft grass in the breeze.

"Evie," he tried again. "Come on. It's time to go in. Let me help you down."

What should he do? Tonight he'd seen a new side to Evie, one he hadn't even known existed. The woman had a sassy tongue when she wanted one. He couldn't leave her out here, but it was evident she wanted nothing to do with him. Well, that was just too bad. "We're both tired and it's been a

long day. You're making this more difficult than it has to be."
Without waiting for a reply, he scooped her up in his arms,
expecting her to fight him, or push him away.

Instead, she melted against his chest without saying a
word. Her face tucked in under his chin and he felt the
wetness of her tears against his neck. His anger evaporated.
He thought he smelled something sweet, like chocolate, but
then it was gone.

He crossed the yard and took the stairs two at a time.
He carried her over the threshold into the cold, dark house,
wondering how he was going to light the lantern and start the
fire with her clinging to him this way.

"Sorry about the house being cold," he said, looking for
something to say. "I stayed outdoors most of the day, tending
the cattle and cutting hay."

Truth was, he'd caught himself all too many times
starting for the house, intending to see Evie, be with her, enjoy
when her cheeks blossomed as he told her he'd never seen a
bed so properly made, or brighter windows than hers. Then
he'd remember she was spending the day with Hayden and
Ina, and his mood soured, and his heart felt like a stone.

He stopped in the middle of the room, but she made no
move to leave his arms.

"Evie," he said gently, starting to get worried. "I need to
go out and stable the horses."

Again when she didn't respond, he carried her into the
bedroom and laid her on the bed. She kept her eyes closed,
even though they both knew she wasn't asleep.

"Okay, then." He looked down at her. Brushed several
wisps of hair out of her face. "I'll be back in a few."

He turned and left, not knowing what else to do. He
missed the feel of her pressed up next to him, clinging to him.

Whether she liked it or not, liked the country or not, they were wed. Maybe it was time he let her know that she was his.

Hurrying in the barn, he unharnessed the team and turned them out. He was just about to button the place up when he spotted something in the buckboard behind the seat. The basket Evie had brought home with her from the Klinkners'. He'd forgotten all about it. Circling to the passenger's side, he lifted it out from the bed of the wagon and looked inside. At first, he couldn't tell what it was. There was a balled-up piece of yarn with knitting needles, and he figured the two women had started some project together. Underneath that, before he could get to it, a savory aroma wafted up, making his mouth water and his stomach gurgle painfully.

Chapter Twenty-Four

Evie lay on the pine-posted bed, tired, despondent, and more than ready to give up on everything. If he wanted her to leave, she would. Living with a man who didn't want her was too painful. She listened, wondering if he was going to return. He'd said he was, but that didn't mean he wouldn't ride off, leaving her to clear her things out. Mentally squaring her shoulders, she sat up, wiped her eyes. God willing, she'd get through this, same as her mother had when she found herself with child.

She swung her legs over the side of the bed and went through the dark house to the hearth in search of the small box of matches. With shaky hands, she lit the lantern on the table, and when light blossomed, she felt a little better. She lit two more, then stacked some tinder in her oven and wadded up some old newspaper. Lighting it, she put the teakettle on, then remembered the food in the wagon.

Boot heels sounded and the door opened. Chance stood there with Ina's basket in his hands. He walked to the table and set it down. "Found this in the buckboard."

"Thank you."

For several long moments, he just stood there, watching as she took the containers out and set them on the table.

Potato salad, slaw, and more than enough fried chicken to feed them both for a couple of days. Ina had also given her a loaf of fresh bread to add to the fare. She arranged them on the table, then fetched two plates and set them on her pretty white tablecloth.

"Aren't you going to remove it?"

She usually took the cloth off, wanting to keep the linen tidy, but what did it matter, really? "No. Not tonight."

He went to the sink and worked the pump, and she could hear him washing his hands.

"Looks like you and Ina were busy today," he said over his shoulder.

He sounded different. Why? She had no idea.

"We did some cooking to pass the time."

At the table, he pulled out her chair and just stood there.

"Thank you, but I'm not quite ready to sit. You go ahead and make yourself comfortable. I'll get the tea and butter for your bread."

"That's all right. I'll wait."

Darn! He was making her nervous. She wished he'd just sit down and eat. Take his eyes off her every move.

Finally finished, she took her seat and he gently scooted in her chair. She served their plates, said a silent blessing. Nothing looked appealing. After the day she'd had, cooking, nibbling and tasting, separating eggs, chopping onions, and then the argument on the ride home, she had no appetite at all. Chance dug in heartily, however, seeming to enjoy every bite he took.

After a few minutes of silence, he took his napkin from his lap and wiped his mouth. "This is really good." He looked at her. "You made it?"

She nodded. "We made it together."

"Sure is welcome after a long day of work." He took a gulp of tea from the mug Faith and Amy had given them. He forked half a chicken breast onto his plate and started cutting. "I've been thinking. We could use a hen house. That way we'll have fresh eggs and maybe even a supper like this once in a while."

Just like that, he'd snapped out of his mood? The black cloud hanging over his head since their walk in the moonlight last night, gone, vanished from just a few bites of fried chicken? Really?

He looked at her. "What do you think? Wouldn't take me long once I got started."

What? She wanted to pour out her heart. Tell him her whole past; get everything out on the table. Tell him and have him love her anyway. Pledge his soul to her, through good times and in bad, through misunderstandings, feelings of anger, sadness, and joy, through anything life could throw their way. But now, fried chicken and potato salad meant more to Chance than whatever had ruined two whole days of their life. Her heart squeezed painfully, and a small hitch in her breathing drew his attention.

She didn't understand it. Didn't understand *him*. Her husband, a stranger. "Sounds fine. I'd like that."

"We'll put the henhouse on this side of the barn," he said, totally unaware of the war her heart was waging inside her chest. "So we can keep an eye on the flock. Make sure no coyotes get in and cause trouble."

"That would be nice." What else could she say?

Dexter scratched on the door. She started to get up to let him in, but Chance stopped her with a hand on her arm. "He can wait. You need to finish your supper."

And so the evening went. All the joy of her learning to bake and cook for her husband was gone, and Chance tiptoed around her as if he thought she would break. She shrank into herself when he lit a fire and pulled a buffalo robe close to the hearth. The only chairs they had were the ones at the dinner table, and not very comfortable for relaxing. Chance several large animal skins stacked in the corner of the room and they had, on occasion, used them to sit by the fire. Either she read aloud or they talked. Tonight, she didn't feel that invitation at all. She quietly went about washing and drying the dishes, then putting them away. Occasionally she'd glance at him where he sat, lost in thought, feet stretched out toward the flame.

"Good night," she said softly, standing by the bedroom door. She held the lantern from the table, leaving him the light of the fire and one other small lamp on top of the pie safe Roady had built.

"Good night. Sleep well." He didn't turn, or smile, and the sorrow in his voice was as thick as the spring grass on the rolling hills outside.

Inside the bedroom, she clicked the door softly closed, not knowing what else to do. Chance's bedroll was where it always was, still rumpled from last night's sleep. Would he come in later? She didn't think so. Everything had changed, and she wasn't sure of the reasons why.

She placed the lantern on the secondhand dresser Chance had surprised her with, and opened the top drawer. Next to her stationery was her feather duster, lying there innocently as if it were nothing more than a pretty sachet, a knickknack to keep. Pain ripped through her already tattered heart. In actuality, the seemingly innocent instrument brought her past life rushing back, her secrets along with her pain. It felt as if the thing was mocking her for actually believing her possibilities for change—for a family and love—might actually happen.

She pushed the duster aside and took a piece of her stationery, sadness for what could have been weighing her actions, and put the paper next to her small bottle of ink on top of the furniture. Sitting on the bed, she carefully dipped her pen. Her hand shook so violently she had to stop and compose herself or Trudy wouldn't be able to read a word. She needed to tell someone her heart was breaking, her world turning upside down, and ask how to save her crumbling life. She began, *My Dearest Trudy...*

Chapter Twenty-Five

Rising early, Evie found Chance's bedroll on top of the buffalo robes before the hearth. Sometime during the night he'd come into the bedroom. She knelt down and ran her hands over the soft blankets, missing her husband dearly. How had things gone so wrong, so fast? She held one blanket to her cheek and closed her eyes. Imagined Chance's face the first time she'd seen him at the stage. What could she do?

With a sigh, she stood. Turned. Something on the table caught her eye, something that hadn't been there when she'd gone to bed. Hurrying over, she found a pair of trousers and a boy-sized shirt neatly folded. She held them up, then measured each piece to her body. A whisper of hope lightened her mood, causing a slight smile to play around her lips. *Maybe he does care.*

She went to the window and searched outside, hoping to catch a glimpse of him. Thank him for his thoughtfulness. She wondered when he'd purchased them. Yesterday? When he'd been so withdrawn?

The barn seemed quiet. Going out on the front porch, she looked around, took in the rolling green pastures and clear blue sky. Nothing. No one. Not even Dexter.

Feeling lonely, she washed and dressed in her new clothes. They felt strange over her corset—a bit loose—but were soft and comfortable. She peered into the mirror hanging on the wall.

She looked like Ernie, her friend in St. Louis who came to trim the trees! She turned first to her left and then to her right. Hopped up and down. Lunged forward, then back. Wonderful! She liked them. How easy it would be to scrub the floor and shake the rugs. She imagined herself in the field, cutting hay alongside Chance.

Bringing her thoughts back to the moment, Evie felt a burning desire to send her letter on its way to Trudy. Maybe her friend would have some wisdom to help. The thoughtfulness of the clothes inspired hope, but didn't mean Chance had changed his mind.

Perhaps she could handle mailing the letter herself. The other day, on their way to town, Chance had shown her a sturdy wooden box nailed to a tree, a short ways past where their wagon path met the main road. The box had a door and a latch, which kept out the weather. Next to the container was a little pointy sign that read, Y KNOT, 3 MILES. He'd said she could leave letters there if she wanted. A rider made the rounds every few days and would gather anything left inside. At the store, Mr. Simpson posted the mail and kept a tab to be paid later. If a neighbor came by on the way to town, they'd pick up any posts and drop them at the mercantile. She shouldn't send money, of course, or anything of value, but letters would be safe because the law prohibited anyone tampering with the mail. *A fact I know well enough now!*

If she didn't try now, it may be days, or even a week, until she could post her letter to Trudy.

The house was already tidy, and there were still leftovers from yesterday for a noon meal for Chance, if he came in to eat. So, letter in hand, she started down the strip of land between the wagon ruts, her boots silent in the soft grass. She'd make it to the drop box and back before being missed.

Chance straightened, removed his hat, and swiped his arm across his sweaty brow. The cool breeze felt good as he leaned on the shovel and looked at the large hole before him in the soft, fragrant earth. The lifeless body of a tiny heifer calf lying on the grass nearby made him swallow hard. The mother grazed over the rise, every now and then giving a sad *moo* as if wondering what had happened to her young'un.

What a shame. He was moved by the tininess of the animal, its delicately soft hide, its big, sleeping eyes. Well, he knew the calf wasn't really asleep, but liked thinking that rather than the alternative. Why, was a mystery. The cow looked fine. Her milk had come in and she didn't show any signs of a problem. Maybe the little one had something inside that hadn't developed enough.

Such was life. He pressed his hat on, took up the shovel and resumed the work, hefting a load of dirt out of the hole and depositing it neatly alongside.

Life and death. Good and evil. Love and...*pain.*

He reined in his thoughts. Who could understand any of it? Evie popped into his mind and he shook his head dispiritedly. She confused him. He'd thought he was ready for a wife, but now he wasn't quite so sure. Getting married wasn't like breaking a new horse. Horses were predictable. Once you trained them and got used to them, they were loyal and responsive. Heck, he loved his horses. And, sadly now, he loved his wife, too. But she was a different story altogether. "Training," if that's what he was supposed to be doing, wasn't going so well with her. He couldn't figure her out. Was she happy? Would she stay true to him? Why would she want a whole day with Ina? Should he trust what she said?

Maybe he'd been a fool to get so riled when she asked to see her friend in Y Knot. But anything dealing with Hayden Klinkner had him seeing red. If Evie hadn't wanted to go back to St. Louis before yesterday, she surely must now.

Finished digging, he put the shovel down and carefully lifted the tiny animal in his arms, a burn stinging his eyes. He couldn't help it. He loved his cattle. Every single one of them. He gazed at her face, the dark black line outlining her eyes and muzzle. Her tiny little hooves clicked together, making Dexter look over from his spot in the grass.

As he placed her gently in her grave he dashed away a tear. "Here you go, pretty little one. Rest well." He thought of Evie last night in his arms, despondent, her wet cheek against his throat. Her pain. Her sad voice. His first tear was followed by another and another, until his face was wet. How could he have treated her so badly?

Drawing his handkerchief from his pocket, he blew his nose and got back to work. After the grave was filled, he covered the mound with several large rocks and dragged over some deadfall to protect the small carcass from predators. Mounting Boston while holding the shovel, he started for the house. Mama cow picked up her head and watched him with large cocoa-colored eyes. She swished her tail, twitched an ear. Her lonely moo echoed his own feelings. After a moment, she lowered her muzzle back to the grass and resumed grazing.

Evie strolled along the wagon trail, letting her problems ease away like birds flying off into the sky. She took a deep breath of air into her lungs. Clean and fresh, it went straight to her heart. How could anyone feel down on a day as beautiful as this? The tails of her cotton shirt bobbed around her hips and she'd had to roll the cuffs of her trousers so they wouldn't drag. But boy, were her new garments comfy. Without the yards of fabric swishing around her legs, she felt free and alive.

She'd traveled a good thirty minutes. She was so far out now, she couldn't see the homestead. From her couple of trips into town, if her memory served her correctly, it wouldn't be long before she reached the drop box.

That thought led her back to her quiet ride home last night with Chance. The resigned tilt of his strong jaw. The letter in her hand suddenly felt heavy. Had she overreacted by sending this too soon? Maybe she was exaggerating. Maybe Chance hadn't felt well the last couple of days. Perhaps men were more different than she realized. Moody. Temperamental. She really didn't have anything to compare him to. Whatever the reason, she was tired of trying to figure him out. The exertion, change of scenery, and the wind stirring the trees had lifted her spirits so much she wondered if she had made something out of nothing. Next week Ina had promised to teach her how to make a roast with all the fixings, sure to melt any man's heart. Perhaps she had better get over there today.

"There," she said aloud. "That wasn't far at all." Several trips up and down the stairs in the Victorian required more exertion.

No sooner had she checked the box out thoroughly for any sign of creatures, webs, or scary things, and closed her letter inside, than the sound of thundering hooves pounding her way brought her head snapping up.

Twirling around, she found Chance barreling down on her as if demons were on his tail. His horse flew over the ground as Chance leaned forward over his neck. He reined the gelding to a stop and swung from the saddle. In two strides he was at her side, wrapping her in his arms. When she tried to pull back so she could see his face, he crushed her to him.

She pushed on his chest, straining to get a breath of air. "Chance, what is it?"

He trembled, but stayed silent, holding her close and making all the worry and pain from yesterday dissolve into a mist of happiness. Whatever had changed his heart, she was so happy she felt weak. "What?"

His arms finally loosened and he took a step back, letting her see his face. The reins of his horse hung limp in his fingers.

Dexter, his tongue lolling from the side of his mouth, finally caught up. The dog's expression was one of pure indignation at being taxed to his limit. He flopped on the grass and promptly closed his eyes.

"Chance? Tell me this instant."

"Nothing. Just found you gone. Wasn't sure if you'd finally—" He stopped. Looked away.

"What?"

"Packed up and left."

She couldn't understand why he'd think that. "My things are all still in the house."

"Once I found you gone, I didn't take the time to look. Just jumped on my horse and followed you."

She reached up and touched his face, tenderly. Were these tears?

He tried to look away.

"Chance?"

"I…" He swallowed and looked into her eyes. "*We—*lost a calf sometime last night."

The wind blustering in the trees, and Boston's labored breathing were the only sounds.

"I'm so sorry, Chance."

"That's not the only reason," he said, emotions clouding his face. "I couldn't live if you left me, Evie." He cleared his throat. "I just couldn't."

What a wonderful, complicated man she'd married! He was granite hard and as tough as nails—but could shed a tear over love. Her hand lingered, cupping his cheek. "Chance," she whispered. "I'm sorry for whatever I've done. I'd never want to hurt you. Or make you angry as I did yesterday. All I want is to be your partner, take care of you, be a help, not a hindrance. But mostly, and from the bottom of my heart, for now and for always, I want to be your wife, the mother to your children." Her face warmed as she prepared to say what was really in her heart. "I want to be your love."

Chapter Twenty-Six

Chance's eyes pierced hers hungrily. He wrapped her in his arms and pulled her close. As his lips lowered, she realized for one enticing moment that he was going to kiss her. Flames ignited between them that had nothing to do with the weather.

Tingles raced through her body, marking her, changing her, stealing her breath. He tasted of wind and sun and broken hearts. His kiss asked for forgiveness, loyalty, love. She felt his regret over their argument—regret as strong as her own. When his lips ventured down to taste her neck, heat like warm, flowing honey, seeped into her veins. Daring chased away her skittering heart and she tipped her head back boldly, giving him greater access.

"I'm sorry too," he said against her neck, then took a breath. He spoke so softly she thought the sound might have been the wind. "I—" His voice faltered. "I got crazy jealous over you spending time with that Hayden Klinkner. Made up all sorts of foolish stories in my head that you'd gone over to Ina's to see him."

Evie couldn't stop her small gasp of astonishment. "No!"

A moment passed. She gave him a little shake, pulling back just far enough to see one corner of his mouth twitch up and his color deepen. "Are you serious?"

"Yes," he said sheepishly. His hat was like a canopy, shielding them from the world. His eyes dropped to her mouth and her insides flamed, hungering for something she'd never had. She went up on tiptoe, boldly pressing her lips to his, loving their warmth, softness, and most certainly not ready to relinquish this intoxicating man. "I'd never do a thing like that. I'm *your* wife, Chance Holcomb. It will take a lot more than that man to get rid of me."

Right then a gust of wind rocked his hat and, in a gale of laughter, they both reached up to stop it from sailing off.

Dexter, refreshed from his short nap, pranced between their legs as if not wanting to be left out of the fun.

"Storm's coming." Chance looked up at the sky, then back toward the ranch. He still held her in his arms. "We should probably get back."

She nodded, liking the way his gaze warmed her face, melted her insides. A smile pulled at his lips. Just as he drew her close and lowered his head for another kiss, a crackling light flashed over the mountains, breaking their union. A low, deep rumbling from afar warned of the approaching tempest.

Indeed, dark, brooding clouds had replaced the fluffy ones she'd enjoyed on her walk here. They glided across the sky like the massive seagoing schooners she'd read about in a picture book in Mrs. Seymour's library. It was amazing how fast the weather could change. Another gust sent leaves and small twigs up against her legs, and Boston danced around nervously. Still, she was loath to give away the closeness she felt at this moment. Wanting to keep his attention, she dropped a curtsy, then pivoted slowly. "How do I look in my new clothes?"

He stepped back and folded his arms, looking her up and down.

"Chance?"

"Like a rascally little boy."

She laughed delightedly. He went over to his horse and lifted the stirrup, checking the cinch. "We should get going. Storms in Montana are nothing to fool with. They move fast and furious."

A lump of fright wedged in her belly when she realized he was waiting for her to mount the horse. She didn't know how to ride. She liked horses well enough—but from the other side of a fence.

"I'd prefer to walk," she said, taking in the animal's large, muscular chest and hips. Boston tossed his head, his reddish brown coat glistening in what was left of the sunlight.

Chance's hawk-like gaze zeroed in on her. She reconsidered.

"I'll run," she offered.

"No, you won't." His voice was stern. "Lightning has found smaller targets than you. Come on, we need to get back." He held out his hand, not asking but telling.

She inched forward, her mouth suddenly dry. "I've never ridden."

"Doesn't hurt too much when you fall."

"Chance!" She stepped back out of arm's reach.

"I'm just kiddin'. I won't let anything happen. As a matter of fact, I'll put you up front where you'll be as safe as a babe in a carriage. You'll have a nice view, too." He ran a soothing hand down the neck of his agitated gelding.

The horse pawed the dirt, his nostrils wide.

"Boston is young, but as solid as they come."

When Chance lifted a brow and drilled her with a no-nonsense, get-moving stare, Evie inched over to the side of the horse.

"Grab hold of the horn."

"Chance, I don't know. I read that horses know when—"

She gasped when his hands grasped her middle. Before she could say another word, he lifted her up and she instinctively swung her leg over the back of the horse. He plunked her in the middle of the saddle. The worn leather was slippery but more comfortable than she'd expected. It seemed like a mile down to where Dexter watched, tongue out, tail wagging.

What an unladylike position! What would Mrs. Seymour say?

"Chance." Her voice wobbled. She swallowed down a lump of fear.

"Here I come, Evie. Scooch forward."

"Horses can feel when a person is frightened, Chance! Well, I'm frightened now! I want to—"

"Stop jabbering. That's the only thing Boston ain't gonna like." He slid his boot into the stirrup and swung aboard behind her, squishing their bodies intimately together and pushing her even farther forward in the saddle. She snapped her mouth closed and tightened her grasp on the horn.

The horse wheeled around easily, and they started toward the ranch. The wind had picked up and was now beating down the grass and bending the tops of trees. They slowly picked up speed until it felt as if they were flying. The ground raced past. The pounding hooves sent fear into her heart. *I don't want to fall!*

"Look there," Chance said close to her ear and pointed north.

The whole horizon was black. She couldn't tell where the mountains ended and the sky began.

"It's a bad one. I'm glad I found you when I did. You don't want to get caught out in a storm like that."

"Will we beat the rain?" she asked, nearly shouting to be heard over the storm.

"I hope so!"

"What about the calves?"

"They'll stick close to their mamas. Can't bring 'em in every time bad weather hits. Hold on now, we're gonna gallop."

Chance kept one possessive arm protectively wrapped around Evie's middle as they galloped toward the ranch. He bent his head into the wind to keep his hat. This morning the crisp air had hinted of rain, but now the intensity of the skyline surprised him. Tonight would be a doozy. A good test for the house. And barn. A good test for Evie too, although he wouldn't let her be hurt. This would be a trial run for when winter came.

Evie's body, cuddled in front of him made him realize just how strongly he felt for her. Still, shame ate at his gut. How could he have thought she'd run off, just as his mother had long ago? He closed his eyes for a moment then released a long sigh, relaxing in the saddle and enjoying the powerful motion of his horse. The feel of his bride in his arms. He was tired of being angry with his mother. Maybe it was time to forgive and forget.

A large raindrop splashed the crown of Chance's hat, bringing him back to reality. First a sprinkle, then smattering. Then, in one ominous moment, the sky darkened and the cloud above opened up and let go its burden, drenching them as they galloped over the land.

A bolt of lightning lit the sky. Evie stiffened, but if she'd made a noise he hadn't heard over the pelting rain. The light sizzled across the horizon from east to west, lighting everything around.

"Hold on," he shouted close to her ear. She hunkered down close to the horse's neck as they dashed over the slick earth. The deafening boom that followed rocked them, sending Boston leaping wildly sideways in a burst of fright.

"Easy, now," Chance crooned to the horse—and Evie—as he pressed Boston with his legs and collected some rein until he regained control of the animal.

The house appeared ahead out of the darkness. He slowed his horse to a lope, then slid to a halt not far from the porch steps.

He slung his leg over the saddle, stepped to the ground, and then reached for Evie. She was drenched and shaking, her hands gripping the saddle horn with a vengeance.

"Come on, sweetheart." When she wouldn't let go, he carefully peeled her fingers away, pulled her off Boston and, in spite of the downpour, held her until she was steady on her feet.

Boston jerked the reins and the wind howled. Dexter ran up the porch and stood by the door shaking, wanting out of the storm.

Leaning close, he shouted, "Get into the house and into something dry. I'll be back shortly."

She gasped and gripped his shirt when another bolt of lightning split the blackness, lighting the sky above them. "Where're you going?"

"The barn. I need to get the horses inside. Won't take me long. Go on, now." He waited until she was up the steps and through the door, making sure she was safe.

It took a few minutes to get Boston unsaddled and rubbed down, and to bring in the other two spooked, wild-eyed horses. Chance slung an armful of hay into each stall to keep their minds off the storm.

He entered the house and shut the door, closing out the tempest, then stripped off his wet coat and hat, and hung them up. When he turned, his breath caught. Evie had changed into a formfitting black skirt that showed her slim figure much better than the denims he'd bought her, and a shirtwaist with a pretty lace collar and cuffs. Her feet were bare as she moved around the kitchen. Her hair, flowing loose and still a bit wet, glimmered in the soft light. She'd gussied up for him. Even after that wild ride. She, too, felt the specialness of the moment. The happiness in her eyes vied with the lantern glowing on the table.

She looked enchantingly beautiful, and confident. A band of love squeezed his chest, and he couldn't look away.

Chapter Twenty-Seven

"**Y**ou be sure to take off those muddy boots," Evie said, trying for a playful tone. "I did the floors yesterday and don't feel like another go-round this soon."

"Yes, ma'am," he replied, toeing them off and setting them neatly next to hers.

Something in his voice drew her attention. She swallowed. Focusing, she laid five freshly washed potatoes on the cutting board and began slicing them into thin sections—just as Ina had taught her. She'd already placed a skillet on to warm, with a large dab of butter melting inside. She fumbled the large knife and a slick potato chunk skittered across the floor in Chance's direction.

He bent over, picked up the spud, and approached her slowly like a wolf zeroing in on its prey.

Their eyes met and held. Chance's intensely sensual expression sent her heart skittering in her breast. There was no doubt what he was thinking.

"An escapee," he said, his voice low and sensuous as he placed the piece of potato in her waiting hand. All the while, his eyes wooed her insistently.

Unable to break the spell or calm her breathing, she felt her face flame. The driving rain buffeting the window echoed the tension flaying her insides, winding her nerves tight like a spring. His fingers lingered in her open palm, sending a burst of pleasure to the pit of her belly.

"You go ahead and clean up," she whispered, thinking how handsome he looked with his rain-tousled hair over his forehead and the wet, chest-clinging shirt. "I've put a pitcher of fresh water for you in the bedroom. Supper will be ready shortly."

We are man and wife. There was nothing wrong or shameful with her racing, wanton thoughts, or her driving need. She wanted him. Tonight. Plain and simple. She prayed he felt the same.

Waiting any longer would be foolish when she ached to fall into his arms and give herself to him completely. She had known from the moment she'd said "I do" that "she really, truly *did*". She'd fallen in love with Chance! From his letters, his sincerity, his golden heart. Now that the problem between them had been worked through, she felt there was nothing in the world that would ever again get in the way of their happiness.

A scratching at the door broke the spell. "Dexter!" she cried. "Hurry. He's probably scared to death."

"Thought he came in with you?"

"He did. But then he wanted out when he realized you'd gone to the barn."

Chance opened the door.

Dexter bolted in just as a flash of lightning brightened the front pasture, making her jump. A heart-stopping crack of thunder followed immediately, shaking the walls.

"Much too close for comfort." Chance glanced out the window. "I'm glad I had the sense not to build under the tree."

He chuckled, then added, "But the storm's moving fast. The worst will be past soon."

She took a deep breath. "Good. Now go on and get changed. I'm sure you're hungry."

He nodded and his expression softened, his gaze dropping to her mouth. He kept it there so long she thought she might faint right away. "I am," he said, the words slow, ripe with meaning.

She swallowed and felt the color rising in her face. Without another word, and much to her relief, he disappeared into the bedroom, Dexter following behind.

She dashed into action, scooping the potatoes into her hands and dropping them into the hot skillet. She jumped back when they popped and splattered. A warm, buttery scent filled the air. Not wanting them to burn, she pushed the hot pan over the flat-top to a spot of the stove that wasn't directly above the flame. Quickly, she unwrapped the chicken pieces from last night and stirred them into the potatoes, figuring cooking them again couldn't hurt. Cooking was a welcome challenge now. One she didn't fear. And, what else? What else did she have to experiment with?

Chance stepped out of the bedroom with one thought on his mind. As hungry as he was, even the mouthwatering aroma wafting from the stove couldn't divert his ravenous need for his wife.

She stood with her back to him. Didn't hear as he crossed the room in his bare feet. A squeal of surprise issued from her lips when he scooped her up into his arms, at the same time scooting whatever was cooking off the stove. Her eyes opened wide, and the tip of her tongue slipped out to moisten her lips—a good sign! She circled his neck with her arms, adding fuel to the inferno burning inside him.

He lowered his head. Took his time to caress her lips, make his intentions known. He hoped she would say yes. Forget the waiting. Two weeks living with Evie was enough to test any man's mettle. Her lips, sweeter than any wine he'd ever tasted, were velvety soft. He ventured to her ear and neck.

She whimpered softly, wriggled, pulled him closer.

"Evie," he whispered next to her ear. "I want to make love to you. Hold you in my arms until the moon crosses the sky and the morning comes. Sweetheart, do you know what I'm asking?"

She looked up into his face with passion-filled eyes. She nodded. "Yes, I understand. I love you, Chance. I want to be your wife in every way."

She looked so achingly beautiful, he couldn't tear his gaze away. Two weeks ago, he'd once thought meeting Evie at the stage was the most important moment in his life. Now he knew different.

"Fine then, me too." He took two strides and stopped under the doorframe. "Look up."

She did. They stood in the doorway to their bedroom, rain and wind buffeting the windows, lightning outside giving them a show. "I didn't get to carry you over the threshold when you first came out. Last night I did, but you were sad, and so was I. Therefore, I'm doing it again now. For good luck. And until the end of time. I'm the luckiest man in the world since the day you came into my life."

Evie scrunched her face, then twitched her nose. A persistent tickle above her upper lip made her give a soft snort. Still drowsy with sleep, she slid her hand from under the warm blankets and rubbed her nose vigorously. Stretching, she rolled to her side and opened her eyes.

Chance! Smiling into her face.

With excruciating slowness, her actions of the previous night seeped into her sleep-deprived brain, heating her face. His wily expression said he was enjoying her discomfort very much. She buried her face into her pillow to escape him.

"Good morning, Mrs. Holcomb. It's about time you woke up."

She dared a glance to the window. Daylight. At least midmorning. They'd slept through yesterday's storm and into the next day. "Oh, no!"

He chuckled, and then leaned over to kiss her cheek. "Doesn't matter at all. No clocks here on the Holcomb ranch."

Evie rolled to her back, making sure her blankets were pulled all the way up to her chin. She couldn't be sure, but it felt as if she was totally naked underneath.

"Everyone came through the storm just fine," he said, sitting on the edge of the bed and making it dip.

Her overfilled heart fluttered softly.

"Just in case you were wondering, that is. The barn and windmill are still standing, and every calf is accounted for. In addition, we have a new bull calf. I named him Holcomb's Thunder. Really good conformation. We may keep him."

She'd never seen his face so relaxed and happy. His smile was doing funny things to her insides again, so she tried to distract herself thinking of something—anything—but that was useless. "And I have a pot of coffee all perked and ready to be enjoyed. Can you smell it?"

She could. Her mouth watered, and then her stomach rumbled grumpily for being left empty for so long. But coffee would do for starters. It was just what she needed to clear the cobwebs and wake up her cotton-filled head. "Yes. That sounds wonderful. Would you mind stepping out so I can—"

"Not quite so fast, missy." He leaned over again and began kissing her neck, a spot he'd found last night that she couldn't endure for long before melting completely.

She tried to push him away. "Chance, the coffee…"

"Coffee has the patience of Job here on the Holcomb ranch. It'll be there waiting when we're ready."

Chapter Twenty-Eight

As Evie washed up from the morning meal, she marveled that since they'd become a *real* husband and wife, four days had come and gone in a blink. She never dreamed she could be so happy, so alive, secluded miles away from anyone, just her and Chance at the base of a Montana mountain range. Being a wife, especially to a man like her husband, was more than she'd ever dreamed. She felt like a queen, pampered and loved.

Only one thing marred her happiness. She hadn't told him yet about her past, and how she'd come to have his letters. She'd tried. Two or three times. But every time she began, vowing to trust his love, her courage crumbled. She was desperate not to lose what they'd found. What could one more day hurt? She didn't want to break the spell of such happiness.

Taking the coffeepot from the stove, she poured out the last cold remains, then swished the insides with water. Imagine, he'd brought her coffee in bed every morning, even though she insisted he stop. Last night he mentioned building an indoor room for bathing. He even sat out on a blanket as the sun disappeared behind the mountain and the stars came out one by one—although, the stars were hardly what he was interested in. Her face heated. How he affected her! Chance wasn't anything like the cowboys she'd read about while growing up in St. Louis. He kept her laughing and loving and blessing God for her life.

Each day, after she was finished with her chores, she assisted Chance in whatever he was doing. If that was building, she would hold the tools. If going out to check the cattle, she would ride along—slowly, of course, on Skip, the other saddle horse. Chance always kept her tethered to him with a lead line.

Surprisingly, he'd never complained even once that she'd served him potatoes, in one form or another, every day since. Mashed, fried, baked, mixed with eggs, or made into a sort of sloppy pancake. He brought out venison or beef, adding to the fare, but she needed inspiration. Some new ideas. Tomorrow was the day she and Ina planned for her next cooking lesson, but she dreaded bringing up the touchy subject.

With everything ready, she picked up Trudy's most recent post, the one Chance had retrieved yesterday in Y Knot. She'd skimmed the letter earlier, but wanted to take this time to reread and savor Trudy's news.

Dear Evie,

Well, I have done it! I am married and am now Mrs. Seth Flanigan. Seth is handsome, tall, with good shoulders and a trim waist. I love his unusual eyes. They are stormy gray with a dark ring around the irises. Very dramatic and attractive.

Although Seth was nonplussed by my descending on him with all my worldly goods, including the piano, he took everything in stride. However, the house is now overflowing with boxes and furniture. Much has also been stored in the barn!

Upon my arrival in Sweetwater Springs, I met some very congenial ladies—the doctor's wife, the wife of the minister, and a rancher's wife. I feel as if I have made new friends, although none as dear as you, Evie. I feel we are heart sisters, even though we knew each other such a short time.

We had a beautiful ceremony with red roses provided by Mrs. Cameron, the doctor's wife. Everyone followed us to the farm, where (thank goodness) Seth had stocked up on enough provisions to feed everyone without my having to whip up supper in a strange kitchen with limited supplies.

I will confide in you, Evie, that I am disappointed in Seth's home. I thought I had prepared myself for a simple dwelling, but the starkness caught me by surprise. In the midst of such beautiful surroundings, there are no trees, flowers, or bushes near the house, barn, and outbuildings. Once the kitchen garden is in, I will turn my attention to remedying the situation. However, the beauty of the distant mountains almost makes up for the ugliness of my immediate surroundings. I could gaze upon their grandeur all day.

So far, Seth has been kind and attentive. He has a sense of humor, and I have high hopes for our future. I hope Chance is treating you in a similar manner. But you must write me and satisfy my curiosity!

Trudy Flanigan

(It feels too strange to formally sign myself as Mrs. Seth Flanigan to you.)

Evie sighed. By now, Trudy would have received her letter of distress, the two posts crossing in the mail. She must be worried to death. These last four days with Chance had made her forget everything except him. She needed to write a quick note, even only a line or two, and calm her fears.

"You 'bout ready?" Chance came through the door and went to the table, picked up his coffee mug from the morning meal, and gulped down the last of it. His red plaid shirt looked nice with his light chestnut hair. To her, he was the most handsome man in the world. He looked at her. "What's that?"

"Trudy's last letter. I didn't get to take it all in." Finished, Evie stood. "I'll just go and get my hat."

She was dressed in her dungarees and ready to work. They were taking the buckboard and going over to a place thick with tall, still-green hay. Now that Chance had a herd, he was eager to get some hay stored for the long winter months.

"I'm taking the picnic basket to the wagon, Evie," he called when she went into the bedroom. "I'll meet you out front."

At the mirror, she placed Chance's old cowboy hat on her head. It was a tad big, but worked to keep the sun off her face in the long days outside. Remembering that she was going to be sweating, she opened her top drawer for a handkerchief and rummaged around.

Her feather duster.

Right there before her eyes.

She picked it up, remembering its comfortable weight and feel. Instead of her usual dread, a soft sentiment of love whispered around inside. Those times at the agency had been good days, too. As much as she'd never trade what she had now, she missed her mama and Mrs. Seymour, and being with the brides. The feather duster used to haunt her. Now her heart smiled and she held the implement to her chest, closing her eyes.

At the sound of a throat clearing, she turned quickly.

"Sorry. I don't mean to intrude on a special moment, but I started to get worried when you didn't come out. Everything all right?"

She whipped the duster behind her back, feeling guilty of a transgression. "Yes, everything's fine. I'm looking for my handkerchief. It'll be warm. You, ah, you have the lunch?"

"Sure do. And the blanket."

Her face warmed.

"Well, let's get movin', cowboy," she drawled as she passed him in the doorway. "The sunlight's a-wastin'."

He chuckled at her imitation of him, and followed behind.

Out in the yard, Chance lowered the tailgate and Dexter jumped into the back of the buckboard. The dog sniffed around for a moment before making himself comfortable for the short ride into the back pasture.

Within the hour, Evie was ready for a break. Her arms ached from the weight of the scythe, and she knew her body would be sore tomorrow. She laid the long instrument down in the grass and went over by Chance to watch him work.

"Why do farmers want the dew still on the grass when they cut it?" He'd mentioned the saying at breakfast.

He stopped and looked at her, a healthy sheen on his face. "Good question. It's what my pa used to tell us. He'd say, 'Nate and Chance, we need to get out to the field before the dew is gone.'" He shrugged. "Maybe it was just his way to get my brother and me moving early."

She laughed, loving him so much she thought she might just up and float away.

He took a long drink from his canteen, then slipped its strap back over his shoulders. "Tired?"

"I am. I'm not much help."

"Let's take a break."

"We just got here. I don't want to slow you down." She gestured to the pasture. "You said we need to have this cut by noon, and raked into rows so it can dry before we have to turn it over. That's a lot of work yet to do."

He dropped his scythe and captured her hand. As they walked through the tall green grass, he lifted her fingers to his lips. "You're right. Ranching ain't easy. But you'd never slow me down. I enjoy your company."

"I will if I take you away from what you're doing."

"Hush. I want to show you something."

He stopped and hunkered down.

Being this close to Evie was all he ever wanted. He didn't need anything but her, a roof over his head, and food. All the rest was extra. The last few days had been more than he'd ever expected marriage to be. Plus, she'd surprised him with what a hard worker she was. She was not only his lover, but also his friend, helper, and all-around best companion in the world. His wife could have him laughing or burning with desire from merely a look. He loved her mightily. Until she came into his life, he hadn't known how lonely he really was.

"Look," he said quietly.

"What," she whispered. "I don't see anything."

"Look closer. It's a mama whippoorwill. Her eggs must be hatchin' or else she'd hop away. Try and lure us away from the nest by bending her wing and pretending to be hurt."

Evie gasped softly. "I see her. She's cute. I like her little white speckles."

He thought the bird looked grumpy as all get-out. "Come on. We don't want to disturb her too much."

They slowly turned, then headed back to the hay.

Four hours later, with the tall grass cut and raked into long rows drying in the sun, Chance went to the wagon for the blanket and food, and found Dexter asleep in the back. Like Evie, he looked worn out from the day's activities.

He'd left his wife collapsed in the grass, exhausted. When he'd casually mentioned that there might be a bug or two, she waved him away with a sigh and buckled to the earth. Her hair drooped out from beneath her hat and she'd unbuttoned the collar of her shirt to cool her heated skin.

"Here we go." He shook out the blanket and spread it on the grass.

She didn't move.

"That bad?"

"I won't be able to move for a week. My arms feel like jelly."

"Mmm, jelly sounds good. What do we have packed in the basket?" He rummaged around and came up with two plates of potatoes, some potato salad, and the leftover venison roast.

"I'm sorry, Chance."

"Don't be sorry, everything looks good." It was just a small white lie. He needed to get her into town, so she could go shopping. Maybe pick up another chicken to fry and some more canned goods. His mouth watered remembering the chicken, golden and spiced to perfection.

"I have an idea that I've been tossing around for a day or two. Tomorrow, let's spend the whole day in Y Knot. Do it up right. We can pick up some supplies at Lichtenstein's. You can look at fabric at Berta May's and see if there's anything that catches your eye and, well, we can do whatever you want. The Twilight Singers, a small traveling group, will be performing in the town square gazebo. They come over once a month from Pine Grove on the last Tuesday of each month." He watched as she lifted a forkful of potatoes to her mouth. "What do you say, Evie? We can even have dinner at the hotel. Make it special. I think we've earned a day off."

Her hand stilled midair. Her chewing stopped and her face was turning white.

"Evie?"

She just looked at him, her eyes wide with—distress?

"Evie! Say something! Are you choking?"

Chapter Twenty-Nine

Chance lunged over the food basket and sent it rolling. He wrapped Evie in his arms, intending to shake the potato—or whatever it was clogging her throat—out before she expired. He wrestled her up, feet toward the sky, and began shaking her with all his might.

"Chance! Stop!" Breathless squeals popped out of her mouth. "Put me down!"

It took a moment for her words to sink into his panic-filled brain. He stopped and, still breathing hard, looked down into her red, annoyed face.

"Are you all right?"

She stretched her arms to the ground as he lowered her body. "I will be when you stop this nonsense. What's come over you?"

He felt his face growing hot. "When you didn't answer, I thought you were choking. Did you have something in your throat?"

"Yes, my lunch. But I wasn't in any danger of dying—except from the tiresome fare."

Relieved, but still feeling stupid, he chuckled and sat back down next to her. "Well, if we go into Lichtenstein's, you can stock up on more supplies. My kitchen wasn't prepared for you. We need to change that. Then you'll be able to cook to your heart's content."

There it was again. That look. The one he'd mistaken for fear. What was going on in that head of hers? "Evie?"

"Chance."

If there ever was a tone that marked trouble coming, that was it.

"Yes?"

She just looked at him.

Apprehension zinged through his body, and he rubbed his palms together in an attempt to disperse his runaway thoughts. What could possibly be wrong with a trip into town?

"I—" she said, looking like she might be sick. "I need to tell you something."

Words no man wants to hear. He braced himself. All right, he was up to hearing whatever she had to say. Being her husband, it was his place to be tolerant, and not jump to conclusions. What was this about? He couldn't imagine.

"Best just to get it out quick, Evie. I feel my barometer getting hot with all the things I'm thinking."

She righted the basket and started to put back the few things that had rolled out.

He took her hands. "Tell me, Evie. You don't have to be frightened."

She took a deep breath. "I can't go to town with you because I need to go back to Ina's tomorrow." She stopped, he was sure, to let her words sink in. They were back to that again? Hayden? He'd thought they'd laid that subject to rest.

"Why?"

"Because I can't cook a thing. Ina is teaching me."

He was so surprised to hear her answer, the meaning didn't quite register. He'd prepared himself to hear a heartbreaking story of how she'd fallen in love with Hayden. Something along the lines of inadvertent love at first sight. She just couldn't go on another moment pretending differently, and so on. He shook his head, as if that would make his mind work.

"I wasn't truthful with you in our letters. I let you go on thinking I could cook—but I can't. I'm sorry."

Relief flooded his soul. He felt like shouting hallelujah and doing a cartwheel at the same time. Instead he wrapped Evie in his arms and lowered her to the blanket, kissing her passionately. She tasted salty and warm. Her breathing quickened. His galloped off. Leaving her lips, he kissed a trail up to her ear, and was rewarded with a throaty sigh of encouragement. If he didn't bridle his desires, they might just put on a show for all of nature to see.

She pushed at his chest. "Chance. Did you hear what I said?"

"I did, darlin'." He pulled her up to a sitting position. By her tone, this was important to her. He didn't care if she couldn't cook a lick. That was the least of his worries. He'd teach her himself. He'd be happy to do it as long as she stuck around, making him the luckiest, happiest husband in all of Montana. He wasn't quite sure of how he felt about her spending another whole day at the Klinkners', within easy reach of Hayden, but maybe it was time for him to trust his wife. Believe her words of love and commitment. "I'm listening. I don't see what the big worry is."

"You don't?"

"Nope."

"But you were so angry the last time I spent a day there. What's changed your mind?"

"You."

She just stared at him.

"I guess it's time I shared some things with you. I have a few ghosts hauntin' me now and then. I can't tell you I'll always be this agreeable, but right now nothing could upset me." He could feel his face blooming warm, and his heart started its tom-tom beating against his ribs. He'd never shared his feelings with anyone. He swallowed. Telling her would be harder than he'd thought.

"When I was just a boy, my ma left us. Didn't say why, just up and drove our wagon into town, then took the stage out. She never looked back. Pa told me she couldn't take the solitary life of living so far from a community. We were in Texas at the time."

Evie's expression showed her sorrow.

He didn't want her pity. All he wanted was her love and commitment. For her to be his wife and the mother to the children he hoped would soon arrive. "Don't feel sad, sweetheart. I'm only sharing now so you can understand why I was such a horse's hind end the other day about Hayden. I know he can offer you more than I ever could. Money. A house in town. A life closer to what you're used to. I wouldn't have been able to bear that. The day you went to the drop box, I thought you'd left me like my ma did."

Evie launched into his arms, pushing him down. She embraced him so tightly he wondered where her strength came from. Her voice, clogged with emotion, was shaky when she whispered, "I'll *never* leave you, Chance. I love you more than the earth and the sky and all the stars. Never doubt that."

Her sweet words salved his tattered heart. Taking her face between his palms, he kissed her tenderly, needing to show her just how much she meant to him. "That's good, sweetheart, because I'll never let you."

Chance pulled the buckboard to a halt in the ranch yard. The sun had long since gone and the crickets were singing their songs. Sitting in the middle of the seat, Evie slumped against Chance's side. Dexter sat to her left on the bench, happy to be allowed up front.

Evie's arms were useless. She'd be lucky if she'd be able to move them at all tomorrow. When the buckboard stopped, she opened her eyes and glanced around.

Chance hopped out of the wagon, and the dog followed suit.

"Here we are, Evie," he said. He scooped her up and she didn't resist. Thank heavens her husband was large. Strong. She appreciated that very much at this moment. He set her on her feet before the door.

"What's this?" he said, his voice tired, too.

There was a note pinned to the wood casing.

He took it and opened the door.

She crossed into the cold house.

"I'll get a fire started," he said. "Won't take long to ward off the chill."

"Chance. The note?"

He chuckled. Took off his hat and hung it on the peg. They were both in need of a good, long scrub.

"Just teasing. I could tell by the light in your eyes you're—"

"Chance!"

She looked over his shoulder as he read, "For Evie Davenport Holcomb." He glanced her way and smiled. He didn't know a boulder had just dropped in her stomach.

"Please come into Y Knot at once. You have a woman caller staying at the hotel. Thank you."

Chance was still on the word Knot but Evie had finished silently. Trudy? Had she come to visit after Evie's brokenhearted call for help? Or had Mrs. Seymour tracked her down for committing mail fraud?

He put the note on the table and went over to the fireplace, intent on starting a fire. "A visitor. Do you know who it could be?"

Evie licked her lips. She wasn't sure. She had her suspicions, yes; cold, hard facts, no.

"Evie?"

"I'd think my friend Trudy Flanigan from Sweetwater Springs," she responded softly.

Chance put some kindling in the hearth and balled up a sheet of old newsprint. Lighting a match, he looked her way. "Why? Doesn't that seem a little strange to you that she'd come calling so soon?"

Yes, it did! Why on earth would she do that? Surely, the visitor wasn't Trudy. But if not Trudy, then Evie was in trouble for sure. Was it Mrs. Seymour, with a deputy to arrest her? "It does seem strange. But I think she must be worried about me. I mailed her a letter when I was upset. Thought you didn't want to be married." She swallowed down her fear. Prayed it was Trudy.

"Should we go into town tonight?" she asked. "The note said immediately."

There was no getting around Chance's finding out the truth now. She hoped he would say no to going into Y Knot now. She wanted one more unspoiled night with him. Enjoy the growing bond they'd established. Share a few more hours in his arms before he thought her a liar and a fraud. Her nerves on edge, she went to the sink to light the stove to heat water for them to wash.

"Tomorrow will be soon enough, sweetheart. You're worn out and so am I. Besides, it's late."

It was true. Her heart shuddered. *Maybe too late for me.*

Chapter Thirty

Wearing her pretty yellow dress, Evie wrung the handkerchief she held in her hands as the buckboard rattled along the road to Y Knot. Her nerves were frayed and her mouth as dry as the sand on the road. She'd face her transgressions with a brave heart. Get them out in the open. Clear the air. Thing was, she couldn't bear the thought of living without Chance. Maybe they wouldn't take her away. She had no way of knowing what was going to happen. *Please let it be the Flanigans.* Maybe Trudy's new husband brought her out on a wedding trip.

"You're awfully quiet for someone who has a secret guest visiting. I'd think you'd be alive with excitement."

Chance looked exceptionally handsome in a solid green shirt that made his eyes stand out in his lean, tanned face. Last night, knowing how exhausted she was, he'd massaged her arms and legs, saying how sorry he was for not watching her more closely. After which, they'd made love long into the night.

She'd known this night with Chance might be her last. The thought made the lovemaking bittersweet. To have finally found a love so strong, and a home so perfect, only to lose it

now, almost made her cry. He'd asked why she was so pensive.
She didn't have an answer.

"Whoa, now," he called to the team. He jumped out and
went to her side. Within moments, they were in the hotel.
Chance asked Miss Hallsey, the hotel clerk, if there was a
visitor waiting for his wife.

"Oh, yes," Miss Hallsey said. The young woman looked
at Evie, a smile warming her face. "She's in room twelve. I'll
go tell her you've arrived."

Panicked, Evie turned and looked up at Chance. Why
hadn't she trusted him? Told him everything when they were
alone? Surely it would've been better than this.

His brows drew together when he saw her face. "What
is it?"

Evie couldn't stop her teeth from chattering. Her hands
felt like ice and she had a sudden urge to run out the door.

"Evie? Tell me what's wrong."

"Evelyn?"

The voice came from the top of the stairs. Evie looked
up. Mrs. Seymour stood tall and regal, looking exactly the
same as she had in St. Louis. Had it been mere weeks ago? It
seemed a lifetime.

Chance's arm came around her shoulders as he drew her
close to his side. The room suddenly felt hot, and stale air
closed in on her. Before she knew what was happening,
everything went black.

Chance caught Evie on her way to the floor. He swung her
into his arms and clutched her protectively to his chest.
Whoever this woman was, he'd not let her hurt his wife.

The woman at the top of the stairs gasped. "Bring her up here and lay her on my bed!"

With Evie in his arms, Chance took the stairs two at a time. The woman opened the door to room twelve and he placed Evie on the colorful quilt covering the bed. As quickly as he could, he undid the row of tiny buttons that ran the length of her bodice and pulled back the material, giving her room to breathe. Her eyelids began to flutter.

"Evie, dear," the woman said from the other side of the bed. After Evie's strange response at seeing this woman, Chance didn't know what to think. She was too old to be Trudy, her friend. Was she Evie's mother?

"Evie," he said, softly rubbing her cheeks. He leaned over her small form, thinking how vulnerable she looked. "Sweetheart, wake up."

Miss Hallsey stood in the doorway, wringing her hands. "Would you like me to fetch the doctor?"

"A glass of cool water will do fine," the woman said before Chance could answer. They took stock of each other from opposite sides of the bed.

"Matron?" Evie's voice came out in a squeak.

Matron? He took in the woman's straight back and deep-set, serious eyes. A gray swath of hair at her temple ran through the brown. What was Evie saying? Was this stiff-necked female a matron of a prison? The madam of a brothel?

The woman hurried over to Chance's side of the bed and tried to get close.

But he stood his ground and wouldn't let her near. It didn't matter to him what Evie had done in her past life. He loved her and he wasn't going to let anything hurt her ever again.

"It's all right, young man," she said. "I'm Mrs. Seymour. I've been Evie's employer for many years. I wouldn't hurt her for all the money in the world."

Employer?

He looked down at Evie, who was regarding him stoically. She struggled to sit.

He helped her up, plumping a pillow behind her back. "What's going on?"

Evie looked between them as if deciding what to say. "Chance, this is Mrs. Seymour, from the Mail-Order Brides of the West Agency. I haven't been truthful with—"

Mrs. Seymour put a hand on Evie's shoulder, stopping her. "Before you say anything, dear, I want you to know I appreciate what you did by leaving payment when you left. However, I had to see you. See that you were happy and cared for—and safe." She looked up at Chance and nodded, as if he passed muster as Evie's husband. "I'm more than pleased with my findings. When I return to St. Louis, it will be with a happy heart."

Her left eyebrow rose and she gave Evie a motherly look. "I wish you would have confided in me, Evelyn. Told me what you were going to do. But I completely understand why you didn't."

Evie glanced up at Chance, and when their gazes met, she quickly looked away.

Mrs. Seymour continued, "I can never express how sorry I am that I missed your desire to settle down, to start a family of your own."

"Ma'am?" Evie whispered.

"Please, let me finish. It's important that I do. I hope you will understand that it was my wish to spare you any pain, like what your dear mother endured. I should have realized that I couldn't keep you by my side forever, where I could protect you from the world. It's just not possible. You must live your destiny, taking whatever it is that comes your way."

When Chance glanced at Evie, the waves of emotion crossing her face stole his breath. Guilt, relief, sadness, emerging joy.

Turning back to him, Mrs. Seymour smiled, then patted his shoulder. "And now that I've met your husband, I see sincerity in his eyes as well as in the letter he sent."

The softness in the woman's face made Chance's face heat. She focused back on Evie as she took a letter from her purse and laid the envelope on the bed next to her. "I hope you will forgive me for opening this, Evelyn, but I was frantic with worry. I would have done anything to find you. Along with your money, which I am returning to you, I have a wedding gift of my own for you both. And also, something your mother asked me to keep for you until you married, or until you turned twenty-five."

Unable to stay quiet a moment longer, Chance said, "What exactly is going on here, Evie? I'd *really* like to know." As her husband he had some rights!

A knock at the door interrupted the scene, and the hotel clerk entered, holding out a glass of water. Mrs. Seymour took the glass and handed it to Chance. "I'll wait for you both downstairs." As she left, taking Miss Hallsey with her, she paused just long enough to say, "I liked the buttercup, Mr. Holcomb. It was a sweet touch."

He stared at the closed door for a moment before sitting down abruptly on the side of the bed. Several moments passed in silence.

"I'm not the person you think I am, Chance."

He tried to be patient as she got her thoughts and words together. Truth be told, he was scared to death. "No?"

She shook her head.

"Who are you then?"

"I'm a…"

She swallowed.

There was only one profession she could have had that would make her look so miserable now, as if telling him would be the hardest thing she'd ever done. In a way, it hurt that she was so reticent. He was her adoring husband, after all, and he thought she understood how much he loved her—no matter what. He'd even told her that.

He pictured her yesterday, working hard next to him in the field. She in her boy clothes and his too-big hat. No—there was no way he'd believe it. A saloon girl? And if she were, how on earth had she stayed so innocent and naive? *A virgin!*

"A…"

She looked away.

"Evie!"

"I'm…a *maid*."

"A maid?"

"You know," she whispered. "Dusting and cleaning and sweeping the floors. Washing windows, picking up stray socks, turning down bedcovers." She swallowed again. "At the bridal agency—in the big Victorian house in my picture."

"I thought that belonged to your family."

She looked at him. "Not exactly. When my mama was young, she was a teacher at a woman's university in St. Louis. When she found herself with child, Mrs. Seymour and the Colonel took her in and gave her a job. In that house. When she died, I took over."

Well. That *did* explain her penchant for clean floors, a tidy kitchen, and everything in its spot. Why would she think being a maid was so horrible?

"All right, darlin'. I don't care much about that. I don't understand why you never told me."

She fussed, trying to swing her legs over the bed. "I'm feeling better now, Chance. I'd like to stand up."

"You just stay put until you tell me whatever it is that's making your face so white. I don't like it one bit."

"Well, remember at the wedding I said there were things I should have told you?"

"Go on."

"Well, I snuck your letters without Mrs. Seymour's permission." She took the glass he held and gulped down a swallow and placed it back in his hand. "I *stole* them!" she said forcefully. "I wrote to you, then slipped out under the cover of darkness to travel to you like a thief in the night. Without saying good-bye. Without thanking Mrs. Seymour for all she'd done for me. I'm no better than a cheat and a liar. I don't know why Mrs. Seymour is being so understanding. It's a federal offense to take someone's mail. The sheriff may be on his way right now to—"

Chance belted out a chortle so loud he almost spilled the water.

Evie's eyes popped open wide. "What in the world is so funny?"

"You!"

She straightened her shoulders and looked at him uncertainly.

"And don't *you* remember *me* asking at *our* wedding if you were already married? If you had killed anyone? Or were running from the law?"

She nodded. "Of course I do. I *was* running from—"

He waved her off. "Don't be silly! I don't care about any of that. You're my wife and no one is taking you anywhere. That woman has even said the same."

"There's more."

Relieved and exasperated at the same time, he sighed. "Go on. I feel like this is going to take a while." He was kidding her, but the look on her face said she didn't think it was amusing at all. "I'm waiting."

"You know the girls from the agency are said to be of good moral standing?"

He wanted to roll his eyes. He was hungry. Wanted to get this conversation over with so they could get to the sweet blueberry pie he'd promised her at the Biscuit Barrel.

"Yes."

"I never had a father."

He couldn't help another chuckle from slipping out.

"Chance, this is important. I can't believe you're laughing again."

"I'm not laughing."

"Sounds like you are."

"I'm laughing at your sweetness. Of course you had a father, Evie. Everyone has a father! You're not *that* special."

"I'm trying to tell you I'm an illegitimate child! A bastard! I don't want any more secrets between us. Everything comes out right now."

He could tell this really meant a lot to her. He had to tread carefully. Say what she needed to hear. "You're *not* a bastard. You're my sweet wife. Never call yourself that again."

She looked at him with wide, disbelieving eyes.

"I'm sorry, Evie, that you never knew who your pa was, or that you had a hard life. I truly am. But, darlin', I *love* you."

He paused to let that sink in. "Your background doesn't make a lick of difference to me. I swear I'll make it up to you, though, if you'll let me. I'll love you for me and him both. You'll see. Life will be good. I'll make darn sure of it."

Her lashes dropped over her eyes and she crawled into his arms.

"By the way," Chance whispered into her ear as he held her firmly against his heart. "Since we're having everything out tonight—who's Ernie?"

Chapter Thirty-One

Evie straightened Chance's string tie, his pained expression making her smile. She'd never get used to how handsome he was, or how just a glance from him could steal her breath.

"Tell me again why we had to come to the Klinkners' for my birthday dinner," Chance said through clenched teeth. "I was more than happy just to stay at home. You know how I feel about Hayden."

"You hush. It's going to be fine. I couldn't possibly turn Ina down after all she's done for me. You should be thankful, too, for all the things I've learned to prepare. Besides, the evening will also be a nice send off for Mrs. Seymour. I'm going to miss her when she leaves."

The door opened to both Norman and Ina.

"Come in! We're so happy to have you." Evie followed her friend, pulling a reluctant Chance along behind. Such a stubborn man! Why couldn't he see the night would be over in the blink of an eye.

Hayden, sitting in the parlor with a book open on his lap, stood when they came into the room. Mrs. Seymour smiled her greeting from her spot by the fireplace.

"Chance, Mrs. Holcomb, good to see you," Hayden said, giving Evie a smile.

She felt Chance stiffen.

"Good evening, Mr. Klinkner," she said. She gave Chance's arm a little shake.

"Klinkner."

Evie's nose went up, taking in all the aromas from the dinner she'd prepared with Ina's coaching. Cooking was becoming so much easier, and enjoyable. She'd spent the whole day here, her sense of accomplishment growing with each successful dish. When she was finished with the preparations, Norman had given her a ride to the hotel, where she'd had two whole hours to get ready for Chance, as well as enjoy a good long soak in a hot bath.

After that, Chance picked her up right on time, unlike her first night in town. Around her neck she wore her mother's beautiful drop sapphire necklace. She ran her fingers down the front of the lovely pink floral dress Chance had insisted she buy just for tonight, amazed at its softness. She felt like a princess.

"Dinner is ready," Ina said, bustling them into the dining room. The large round table was draped with a white tablecloth and beautifully set with all of Ina's best china. A bouquet of fresh flowers sat in the center.

"Looks mighty pretty," Chance whispered into her ear. "I hope I don't break anything."

Evie had been gone since early morning and the look in Chance's eyes said he appreciated her effort to make this night perfect. With great care, she'd set the table according to her etiquette book, leaving substantial room for each dish without crowding. She'd arranged the flowers with love, making sure the height wouldn't cut off anyone's ability to converse easily. As the book instructed, she held her head high, in ladylike deportment, and smiled her greeting to the group.

This was Evie's gift to Chance, along with a beautiful woolen dress coat she had wrapped and stashed, hidden away behind the sofa. Her mother's inheritance, that Mrs. Seymour had brought with her, had helped her purchase the present, as well as order a few large pieces of furniture for the ranch house that she waited for eagerly. An overstuffed canary-yellow settee was her favorite acquisition. A brown wing-backed chair for Chance, which he thought much too fancy for a man, and a wardrobe for the bedroom. Oh, and she'd also purchased a butter churn from the mercantile. The remainder of the money she'd put into the bank for a rainy day.

Mrs. Seymour, whose visage now shone with love as she watched Evie play hostess, had surprised them with the beautiful grandfather clock from the parlor of the Victorian. A perfect wedding present that brought back wonderful memories every time it chimed.

Evie's pretty face glowed as she brought out a roasted goose on a large white platter. Carrots, onions, and squash surrounded the bird.

Chance's mouth watered. He could hardly wait to dig in.

After setting the platter in the middle of the table, Evie hurried back into the kitchen for a bowl of dark brown stuffing with little black things that looked like raisins and nuts. Two boats of darn good-looking gravy followed, and lastly—and almost forgotten—she came back with a small serving dish of huckleberry jelly. It was hard to believe she'd done this all for him. Best of all, there wasn't a potato in sight.

All seated, they bowed their heads for a blessing spoken by Norman.

Eating commenced.

"This is the best I've ever tasted, Evie," Hayden said, just as Chance opened his mouth to give her the same compliment. He sat directly across from her. "Darn good."

"Thank you."

His wife was blushing. "It sure is," he chipped in, then reached over and squeezed her hand, running his thumb along the inside of her palm for a fleeting moment. Her eyes widened. "Everything is perfect," he went on. "Matter of fact, I'll have some more of that gravy, if you don't mind."

Chance ate until he thought he'd bust. After supper, they sat in the parlor talking and laughing, him enjoying the feel of his wife by his side. Conversation was lively, with Mrs. Seymour asking a hundred questions about Y Knot and Evie's life here. Evie basked in her attention. He was thankful the woman had made the trip in search of her. Evie's smile hadn't disappeared since after the morning in the hotel.

Every once in a while, Chance thought he noted a wistful expression in Hayden's eyes, almost a sadness. It surprised Chance. The expression wasn't in character for the Hayden he knew. Or thought he knew. Maybe in spite of all his irritating ways, Hayden longed for a sweet wife like his.

"I'll be right back." Evie excused herself, followed by Ina. The two returned, singing "Happy Birthday" at the tops of their voices, as Evie carried in a beautiful chocolate cake covered in tiny white candles.

She held it out to him. "Make a wish, Chance."

There wasn't anything to wish for, except many, many more years with his wife by his side.

He gathered his breath and blew and, for Evie's sake, made sure every single candle was out. Everyone cheered and laughed.

"My wife has really outdone herself again. I've never seen a chocolate cake like this."

The room went quiet. Evie looked away for a moment, then began to laugh softly, followed by the others. What was the secret?

"I'm sorry, Chance," Evie said. "I had to share with the others how from the day we married I've been feeding you potatoes, potatoes, and more potatoes. You've been very kind—though getting a mite tired of them. And now, I hate to inform you, but this chocolate confection is really a potato cake!"

An hour later, in the buckboard on their way home in the moonlight, Evie basked in the memories of the perfect evening she'd given her husband. Chance had one arm around her and held the reins with the other. The love she felt for him was indescribable, so strong and good, and larger than the mountains she loved to gaze at throughout her day.

"Oops, I almost forgot."

She looked up.

He took a letter from his pocket. "I picked this up at the store. From your friend, Mrs. Flanigan."

He pulled the team to a halt and reached back for the lantern. "I'm sure you'll want to read it now, right?" he said, striking a match and lighting the wick.

"Yes, thank you." With eager hands, she carefully opened the envelope and took out the sheet of paper, holding it close to the light. She giggled in a few places. After that came a sniff, a laugh, and a nod.

"Well? You're not going to keep what's making you chuckle all to yourself, are you?"

"All right, here goes. Just keep in mind I wrote to her the night we came home from the Klinkners'. The night I thought my marriage was over. The night you broke my heart into a thousand pieces."

"And the night you stuck your tongue out at me?"

She gasped. "You saw that?"

His arched brow emphasized his no-nonsense look. "You bet I did."

She laughed, then cleared her throat and began reading, moonlight all around, Chance's arm still holding her close.

> *Dearest Evie,*
>
> *It was with surprise and shock that I read your letter telling me of your difficulties with Chance. I am so sorry to hear of his coldness toward you. I wish I were there, so I could give you a heartfelt embrace and more closely question you as to the circumstances of what might have happened, because I sincerely doubt Chance does not want to be married to you.*
>
> *Forgive me, Evie, for writing what may already be known to you. But I know you've grown up without a father or brothers (not that I had brothers) and have little experience with the male sex. Men have the most annoying habit of withdrawing when something is on their mind, and not offering two words about what is wrong.*

Evie poked him in the side. "That's totally true! You can be so exasperating when you're like that!"

"Go on."

> *I remember once when my father had a particularly difficult case, he did not speak to Anna or me for nearly a whole week! Nor,*

when I taxed him about his silence, would he admit anything was out of the ordinary about his behavior!

I also know when I would push him on such matters, to my great dismay, my usually even-tempered papa would often turn surly. Thus I learned to leave him be and go about my regular activities with a cheerful demeanor. Sooner or later he'd return to his normal self.

Therefore, Evie, whatever is on Chance's mind, you must stop questioning him about it. Perhaps matrimony is a greater jolt to his system than he expected, and you must give him time to adjust. He will talk when he's ready. So don't hover over him.

It was his turn to nudge her, hard enough to stop her from reading.

"See. You're supposed to leave me alone when I don't feel like talking. Not go on and on like a chipmunk gone mad."

"Do I go on and on like a chipmunk?" She gave him you-better-take-it-back look.

"No. Now that I think about it, I'm sure that was someone else."

"You'd better say that!"

Instead, focus your mental and physical efforts on making a good home and being the best wife (short of becoming a doormat) that you can be. But also cultivate other activities that bring you pleasure.

Chance interrupted her again when he leaned over and kissed her neck.

"Chance!"

"I can think of a physical effort I'd like to partake in right now that would bring a whole lot of pleasure," he whispered, sending a bolt of desire coursing through her.

"Chance!"

I am glad you're making a new friend. I also advise you to seek out some friendships with ladies who are not so close to your husband.

I must go. I have just prepared my very first dinner for my husband, and I dare not let it burn!

All my love,

Trudy

Chance broke out in a heartfelt bellow, laughing so hard he had to wipe his eyes on his sleeve. "Ladies who are not so close to your husband? Honey, you're the only woman I'm close with."

"Stop that right now, Chance. I meant I couldn't confide in Mrs. Klinkner because you knew her well. This is a touching letter. Trudy is my best friend. There isn't anyone else who knows me as well, or understands me the way she does."

His eyes turned serious. He gathered her to him, and with the coyotes in the background serenading them from the hills, kissed her until her breath caught and her heart fluttered.

"You sure about that, darlin'?"

She ran her hands over his shoulders, loving the feel of him. "Well," she began, "perhaps I spoke a bit too hastily. I guess I'd have to say Trudy knows me *second* best."

With a featherlight touch, she traced his lips with the tip of her finger and watched as his eyes darkened with passion. She wished they were already home. "You know my heart like your own, Chance, and I'm so glad you do."

Acknowledgements

There are so many wonderful people to acknowledge in the creation of this book. First, my good friend, Debra Holland, for coming up with the idea in the first place, one that links our heroines to each other as well as to our respective towns in our individual series. Trudy Bauer to Sweetwater Springs in the Wild Montana Sky series, and Evie Davenport to Y Knot and the McCutcheon Family series—both towns set in the wilds of Montana. Working together has been a joy from start to finish!

My deepest thanks to Jennifer Forsberg Meyer, Leslie Lynch, and Sandy Loyd for the developmental and editorial help. Also my fantastic beta reading team, for their sharp eyes, dedication, and enthusiasm: Jennie Armento, Mildred Robles, Kandice Hutton, Lorna Samboceti Wren, and Mariellen Lillard. Thank you so much!

And, as always, to my delightful readers, who want a story bursting with love and romance, as well as a good horse, a gunfight now and then, and slow cowboy charm. You've filled my life with joy.

Thank you!

About the Author

Caroline Fyffe was born in Waco, Texas, the first of many towns she would call home during her father's career with the US Air Force. A horse aficionado from an early age, she earned a Bachelor of Arts in communications from California State University-Chico before launching what would become a twenty-year career as an equine photographer. She began writing fiction to pass the time during long days in the show arena, channeling her love of horses and the Old West into a series of Western historicals. Her debut novel, *Where the Wind Blows*, won the Romance Writers of America's prestigious Golden Heart Award as well as the Wisconsin RWA's Write Touch Readers' Award. She and her husband have two grown sons and live in the Pacific Northwest.

Sign up for Caroline's newsletter: www.carolinefyffe.com
See her Equine Photography: www.carolinefyffephoto.com
LIKE her Facebook Author Page: Facebook.com/CarolineFyffe
Twitter: @carolinefyffe
Write to her at: caroline@carolinefyffe.com

Printed in Great Britain
by Amazon

16942800R00132